Praise for Wi...
Mackerel

A *New York T...*

"Profits by formidable skill in deft and devious story-telling. . . . The backgrounds here are very real, the characters ring true, and beyond all that, the book is sometimes fall-down funny."
—*The New York Times Book Review*

"This is a tale told by an initiate, full of bounce and flourish, dignifying mystery. Although built on the conventional pieces of mystery thrillers, the plot Weld weaves is inventive enough to keep you guessing. . . . When Weld switches from inside politics to the outside solitude in the book, he leaves behind the typical tone of a mystery to approach real art."
—*Boston Sunday Globe*

"First-time novelist William Weld . . . proves an able stylist in the lively and entertaining *MACKEREL BY MOONLIGHT.*"
—*The Wall Street Journal*

"*MACKEREL BY MOONLIGHT* is a taut, funny look inside corrupt politics and should make you wonder how much of this stuff really goes on. A scary thought. What follows is a highly amusing, but tense, romp through Boston high society, a political campaign driven by spin doctors, corrupt politicians and cops, and an affair with a married woman. The conclusion likely will surprise you."
—*St. Petersburg Times*

"The erstwhile governor of Massachusetts has written a first novel that reads like a script for a Jack Nicholson movie. William Weld is different from the usual author-politician in other ways: Most important, he can write. Also, he feels no obligation to be edifying, only to be entertaining about Boston politics and the wicked who prosper, especially his hero. It's good fun."

—Mary McGrory

"Fast-moving and witty. . . . My test of a good novel is whether I want to keep reading to find out what happens. *MACKEREL BY MOONLIGHT* met the test. No doubt Weld has drawn on his own experiences as a federal prosecutor and successful candidate for office to tell his story."

—*Philadelphia Inquirer*

"A piquant view of American politics from an inside source."

—*Washington Post*

"The guy can really write. There's plenty of juice to William Weld's story."

—*Charlotte Observer*

"Weld writes in a witty fashion with an insider's view of politics . . . [and] finishes this novel with an ending that really surprises."

—*Grand Rapids Press*

WILLIAM F. WELD

MACKEREL BY MOONLIGHT

POCKET STAR BOOKS
New York London Toronto Sydney Tokyo Singapore

A Pocket Star Book published by
POCKET BOOKS, a division of Simon & Schuster Inc.
1230 Avenue of the Americas, New York, NY 10020

Copyright © 1998 by William F. Weld

Originally published in hardcover in 1998 by Simon & Schuster Inc.

ISBN: 0-671-03874-5

First Pocket Books printing September 1999

10 9 8 7 6 5 4 3 2 1

POCKET STAR BOOKS and colophon are registered trademarks of Simon & Schuster Inc.

Cover art by Dan Kirk

Printed in the U.S.A.

To Susan,
the most amazingly good child
I have ever known

Contents

Contents

chapter one

I Get Recruited

Sometimes the good Lord closes one door and opens another.

I was basically fired from my job as a federal prosecutor in Brooklyn, although old Tarzan was too smooth to use that word. Assistant U.S. attorneys do not get fired; they move on to other opportunities. I'll say this for the Justice Department, they bury their dead, they don't leave them out as carrion.

The press had missed the ugly side of the story, but a couple of police reporters were nosing around. I decided the best way to snuff their interest was to get out of New York entirely.

I took a job with Warfield & Coles, a big law firm in Boston. It was far from the best firm in town, but it was Harvard-Yankee "cold roast Boston" all the way, and I craved that. I am underclass Irish, wrong side of the tracks, and I wanted to round out the résumé. I still had thoughts of elective politics. So it was Oak Square in Brighton by night, white shoes on State Street by day.

1

My departure from Brooklyn, like my early life there, was wrapped in secrets. The U.S. attorney was frosted at me because he thought I had obtained some highly visible convictions through overly aggressive (meaning illegal) means, but he couldn't say so publicly, because then the bad guys would get their convictions overturned. This concealment was wildly improper on his part, so he and I both had a motive to keep the whole thing quiet, in fact we have to this day. You have to know how to keep your mouth shut in this business, if you're planning to be in the public eye for a while. And you have to bank on the fact that other people will do the same. So you can never really relax.

It was funny that I got out of town one jump ahead of the sheriff, so to speak, because I had been hanging around with a Reform Democrat crowd and had been thinking of running for district attorney in Brooklyn myself. The police were going to be with me all the way, I can tell you that.

I had an even better secret, too: I actually *deserved* to be fired, though not for the reason the U.S. attorney thought. This was not a factoid I shared with him, or anybody else for that matter. (A factoid is a fact that litigators don't want to admit is a fact, so we call it a factoid.)

My reputation as a maker of high-profile cases was intact when I hit Boston. The only guys that knew my little secret were cops, and you couldn't have better friends than that. I have always loved cops.

When leaving the Brooklyn U.S. attorney's office at the end of 1994, I had taken the standard vow to plead all my future criminal clients guilty and apologize for wasting the government's resources and the court's time. This was a standard joke in the Justice Department. Come to find out, though, the first big criminal case I get in Boston, suddenly I see it's nothing but an overzealous assistant U.S. attorney flinging around allegations of bank fraud like there's no tomorrow, and my guys are simply *misunderstood*. Misunderstood businessmen. So they were trying to make a buck, I say to the prosecutor, so sue them, but for Chrissakes, Pete, this ain't a criminal case and you know it, let's all stop before we do ourselves any lasting harm!

That was my line, anyway. I was careful not to ask my clients too many questions, too. And wrote nothing down. I, uh, maintained my clients' "flexibility." Some unscrupulous and overzealous prosecutors, my former self included, have characterized this flexibility as the ability to lie on the stand without getting caught.

If I do say so myself, I was a good slimeball defense lawyer for that year and a half in private practice. Case in point: as soon as I saw that the government housing inspector had criminal exposure in the Metaxas bank matter, I took my guys straight to the feds. The best advice I could ever give a client is if you're going to break the law, make sure you do it in partnership with somebody more important and famous than you. Someone you can roll over on, at the first sign of rain, in exchange for immunity for yourself. Follow this simple rule, and you will never go to jail. I never had a client go to jail, though I had sent plenty of guys there.

Anyway, my guys walked, twenty-five-thousand-dollar fines, one hundred hours community service, six months suspended, two years probation, even though they were about eight times as guilty as the codefendants, three of whom went to trial and all of whom drew prison time. The HUD inspector got four years.

My phone naturally begins to ring off the hook. My main guy, Mr. Metaxas, Sr., is so grateful he *walks* over to Warfield & Coles a cashier's check for seventy-five grand more than the $465,000 bill I had sent the family. And he's a chirper, so he's telling everybody on the street I can make the sun come out if I want to. Actually, I think it was Pete Croteau just wanting to do a favor for a former brother-in-arms, but I never saw fit to share that view with the clients. Not that my good relationship with Pete was a secret, just that they never asked me. Specifically.

About now I'm feeling pretty good, and in the hallway I actually smile at old man Coles (third generation in the firm), who didn't want me to take the case in the first place because it was criminal. And he says, "Terrence-I-need-to-see-you-in-my-office. Now." Very grave. By the way, nobody calls me Terrence, unless they're joking. My smile goes away.

I go in and there's the whole management committee of the firm. I'll spare you the length of the conversation, but the gist was we can't take the seventy-five K premium, why not, it wasn't billed, so I'll send out a new bill, too late, but the client's happy, doesn't matter it's the principle of the thing. *And* the precedent.

Precedent. Great. They should be so lucky, it happens more often.

So even though my phone's ringing off the hook with new megapocket clients, I'm swearing to myself I'm never going to work for anybody but myself ever again, and one fine morning I get a call that paves the way for just that. With the best of intentions.

It was Detective Lieutenant Rudy Solano, who I had worked Asian organized crime and narcotics cases with in Brooklyn. Rudy was a deer-hunting buddy of mine who had encouraged my interest in politics and was genuinely sorry to see me leave the U.S. attorney's office. He said I was the only lawyer there who thought like a cop, always pressing. Rudy himself was the original hard charger, the most effective investigator I ever saw at finding out when the deal was going down. His arrest and conviction statistics were through the roof. I had loved working with him, even though he was a handful.

Rudy and I were kind of a matched pair, in that both of us were viewed as playing the game near the edge. The reason Rudy's information about deals was so good was that he was literally close to the bad guys, or factions of them, and that made a lot of the lawyers and even some of the cops nervous. Plus, the fact that Rudy was a brash guy who wore gold around his neck made them even more nervous. Personally, I put that down to five parts jealousy and five parts anti-Italian prejudice. There was even a cockamamie story Rudy had had one dealer rub out another, to cover his own tracks on a deal. They never would have spread that around if he wasn't Italian.

Rudy said he wanted to come see me at my State Street office along with a couple of his pals from the Boston Police Department: Jim Fay, the head of the Patrolmen's Union, and Walter St. Onge, the head of the Superior Officers' Association. I said why not. The three of them showed up at ten the next morning, with some snot-nosed kid in tow.

I came out and met them in the reception area, the way I always do. You often get more out of a witness on the way to and from the interview room than you do inside. There's a great scene in the movie *Footsteps in the Fog* where Jean Simmons is at the police station giving phony handwriting samples to prove she didn't write the kidnap note, and they tell her she's in the clear and she's rushing out and they just have her sign the guest register real quick and guess what? It's a perfect match, she's cooked. Misdirection play all the way, she lets her guard down. Beautiful. I love misdirection.

Rudy and I gave each other a one-arm hug. Friendly like, but not too close.

"Still got the gold, I see, Lieutenant."

"Still got the gold, Counselor."

I felt in good company as we padded down the corridor, but I noticed a few arched eyebrows from the secretaries who were accustomed to seeing only pinstripes parade past them, not dress blue. The cops, in turn, were clearly fazed when we turned into my office and they were hit with the full thirty-third-floor panorama of Boston Harbor, Logan Airport, and the harbor islands beyond, curving gracefully into the Atlantic. They grew even more uncomfortable when I invited them to plop themselves down in the four wing chairs that framed the sitting area of my office. It looked as though it was the first ride in red leather for Fay and St. Onge.

Patrolman Fay sucked it in, though, and came right to the point. "It's about the DA's race in Boston next year," he said. "Marty Gross is a good guy, at least he always was a good guy, but lately something's gotten into him. Maybe it's the *Daily Mail*. I don't know. But you can't talk to him anymore. It's like there's this invisible Plexiglas shield."

"He's forgotten his old friends," St. Onge added.

"He has a pretty good reputation," I offered brightly.

"That's because he's eating out of the *Daily Mail*'s hand," said Fay. "He will do absolutely anything they tell him to. That case he brought against O'Brien, the former congressman, was horseshit. It got thrown out by the judge before it got within a mile of the jury, but you couldn't prove that through the *Daily Mail*. All you would know was how 'courageous' Gross was for attacking the so-called Old Boy network. The rank and file knew it stank. They gave Gross the annual Gypo Nolan award at the Mistletoe Society banquet two weeks ago, for being the year's biggest traitor to the Irish cause."

"Gross isn't even Irish."

"You don't have to be, to get the Gypo Nolan award. You just have to be a rat, like Gypo."

"Marty's starting to step all over our homicide investigations, too," said St. Onge. "He wants an assistant DA there before the police even go over the scene. Assistant DA is shaking off the sleeps, giving the girl-friend a little peck on the cheek, meanwhile the perp is in the middle of the next county and blood is dry-ing and we don't have prints we can send to the NCIC computer in Quantico."

"It's like he's so good running the DA's office he'd like to run the department as well. Wants Ditsy trans-ferred as head of homicide, wants Ryan out, wants Miller in, wants McChesney in. What the hell does he know? He's trashing people's reputations who have been in the department for thirty years."

"Okay, I get the picture, I did good in school. Martin's become a politician. Occupational hazard. But I'm a poor humble private practitioner, on his way to being rich. How can I be of service here? I do white-collar defense work. I can't exactly do a criminal inves-tigation of the DA's office."

"We want you to run against Gross in the pri-mary."

This actually did catch me unawares, but I couldn't let them see that, not this crowd. Sign of thickness is as bad as a sign of weakness. So I played for time.

"Great idea, wonderful!" I grumbled. "Blow-in from New York takes on Boston-Chelsea-Winthrop institution, makes fool of self, ruins law practice."

"Look, Terry," said Rudy, speaking for the first time. "It's happened before. Look at that idiot Furbush. He'd been in Queens about three months and he was just standing in the right place at the right time, now he's a congressman. From what I gather, Gross is trying to hang on too long. Three terms is enough for any-body. It's not you, it's the tide."

I took a second or two to chew on this. "I've got no organization," I said.

"You're looking at it." This from Fay. "We'll be quiet. Very quiet. You'll make all the noise. Voice will be the voice of Mullally, hand will be the hand of Fay and St. Onge. Three weeks out, the signs will be there, and bumper stickers, and on election day, every goddamn poll in the city will be triple-manned. Five feet, fifty feet, a hundred feet. Someone comes and chases away the guy at five feet 'cause it violates the election law, somebody else will be right there to come in and take his place as soon as Jack Armstrong All-American is around the corner. Different guy. Jack comes back, it's 'Hey, I didn't know.'"

"I've got no money, no campaign account. Gross has three hundred sixty large in the bank right now, according to the paper," I said.

This seemed to catch the interest of the snot-nosed kid who had been kind of dozing off over in the corner, hadn't even sat down. "As an eleven-year incumbent, Gross should have a lot more in the bank than that," said the kid.

"Besides," said Captain St. Onge, "you're at Warfield ampersand Coles—you're among the rich and famous. Don't tell me you can't raise half a mil in this crowd. Even the secretaries outside have sparklers on, would choke a German shepherd. And we can take care of the rest. Suffolk County isn't like going statewide, it's not totally a media race, it's a pavement race, too."

"I'm prochoice on abortion," I said. "How's that going to go down in Southie and Eastie and Winthrop?"

"No, you're not," the kid broke in. "For these purposes, you are prolife as a matter of conscience. You don't need to say a thing, we'll pass the word. If you ever go statewide, that's a different context, and there will be ample time to review the arguments on both sides of this complex and personal issue."

"I'm sorry, sir, I didn't catch who you were with. Are you with the Police Department?" I asked politely.

Fay cut in: "This is Lanny Green, from the AFL-CIO in Washington. Ran Sam Ward's campaign in the Eighth last year, consulted for Yurkovitch in the Tenth, as well. Knows the terrain in the Northeast upside down and inside out. One of our best young people nationally, if not the best."

"Well, I'm proud to shake your hand again, Mr. Green," I oozed. Actually, I had ignored him on the way in, but I was tactfully burying that error. Lanny smiled, and I knew he had noted this but would never acknowledge it. He had a good handshake for a kid, too. Didn't look over my shoulder.

"Let me come back at you jamokes with a slightly more fundamental problem," I said. "You guys are ticked off at Gross because he's dissing the police and basically high-profiling and hotdogging a lot of stuff, like he's the last guardian of public morals. Am I right?"

"Basically," St. Onge agreed, droopy-lidded. I noticed he had a lazy eye.

"Well, here's the problem. So far as I have any public image at all, or image with the newspapers, whatever, it's the same goddamn thing, if not more so. I personally put away more dirty cops in Brooklyn and Manhattan than anybody except Rudy Giuliani. You want to run a 'regular' against that fella, you got the wrong guy. In terms of how people think about the cops, and who's a 'reformer' and crusader and all that, I'd be perceived as the guy who's going to keep the cops in line, not him. I'd be seen as running to his left, not his right."

Lanny Green allowed a little moment to go by. "Precisely," he said. "*Daily Mail* insurance policy."

It was political love at first sight for me and Lanny from that point on.

"What about Henry Curcio?" I pressed on. "A sitting attorney general who really goes to bat for a DA, feeds him white-collar cases and consumer fraud stuff, can make him look awfully good. I was talking with Curcio at the Columbus Day parade in October, on Bennington Street, and he said Gross was a good friend of his."

"What were you doing at the Columbus Day parade?" St. Onge asked.

"I was marching, with the Ancient and Honorable Artillery Company. I like to meet people. You get to look into ten thousand pairs of eyes, all in one morning, for free. In an approved setting."

"I know you do," said Fay, "or we wouldn't be here. I called Rudy to make the introduction on this, he didn't call me. Your reputation precedes you. Anyway, for that snake Curcio, 'He's a good friend of mine' means he's shooken the guy's hand once. 'He's a close friend' means he's shooken the guy's hand maybe twice. Anybody who really was a close friend of Babyface Curcio, he'd never admit it publicly."

"How are you on the death penalty?" St. Onge asked with apparent foreboding. The foreboding amused me.

"Oh, don't worry about me, guys, I'm okay on the death penalty!" I joked, waving a finger in the air. This was my imitation of a stupid politician. Only Lanny laughed. The others thought I was serious, and that I was trying to duck the question. I saw this and hastily added, "No, I'm just kidding. I'm all in favor of the death penalty, three chairs no waiting, pull the switch myself, lots of walking advertisements out there for capital punishment. Okay?"

"How about changing the law to make it easier for law enforcement to use wiretaps in state court? You know, have more electronic surveillance?" The question came from Lanny, the only person in the room with apparently no law enforcement experience. He offered me a poker face, so I couldn't figure where he was coming from, but I actually knew a lot about the topic.

"Huge issue," I opined pompously. "We desperately need an ELSUR law like the Federal Title III here. It's perfectly easy to do, New York State has it, that's why you see Morgenthau doing corruption cases. Our dumb law is the biggest reason all the corruption cases and the top narcotics cases in Massachusetts go to the

U.S. attorney's office, not to the Suffolk and Middlesex DA's. You can't penetrate that wall of silence without it. They've been trying for years"—I looked at Lanny, whose juvenile features seemed to be forming quite an adult frown—"for years, uh, to get the expansion through the legislature here, and the, uh, criminal defense lawyers have stopped 'em every time. So, great issue for law enforcement, we should be for it." I saw Lanny was now scowling. "Unless," I added, "that's the wrong answer."

"Wrong answer." Lanny exhaled. "Nothing to do with criminal defense bar. In Suffolk County—Suffolk County, *Massachusetts*, as in Charlestown, not Smithtown—it's a constituent issue."

"A what?"

"A constituent issue. Constituents don't like it. Big Brother watching."

"Oh, you mean it's like the *Gazette* printing the daily number backwards, it's just the grease of daily life, it's illegal, everybody knows, nobody cares?"

"Right."

"Uh-huh. Now, not to put too fine a point on it, but suppose I got elected DA, would it be okay if I brought a few criminal cases, or would that offend the sensibilities of the good folk of Suffolk?"

"Relax, Terry, we're just talking about the procedural rules of the game, not substance," said Rudy soothingly. "Everybody's got something on them, some little thing, and as long as they don't get caught in the act, they'd like to think they got away with it, that's all."

"Okay, I'm fine," was what I said. Do you ever know

what you're talking about, was what I thought. But I couldn't risk a smile, so I just looked at Rudy innocently. Sort of like the way Lanny had looked at me.

To Lanny I said, "Very interesting. It seems I have a mix of positions, some are left, and some are right."

"Correct," said Lanny. "And you know why?"

"No, why?"

"Because you're independent-minded."

"I'm independent-minded."

"You think for yourself."

"I think for myself. I . . . I *call 'em like I see 'em!*" I added triumphantly. Lanny nodded, without a smile or a twinkle. This was business.

"Still," I went on, "I'm still not sure I see, what's the angle of attack?"

Lanny drew a single sheet of five-by-eight-inch notepaper, folded only once, from his pocket. "We've been giving that some thought," he said, and tossed the paper in front of me. I read out loud: "'Let's Repeal the Corruption Tax.' . . . Not bad," I said. "And I'll tell you something else. I've had some experience playing that particular fiddle."

"We know that, too," said Lanny.

I rose to my feet, pulling on my coat, and put my right hand in the fold above the suit button, Napoleon-style. "Ladies and gentlemen," I declaimed. "It is high time, it is past time, that we repeal the corruption tax in this city." I grew grave.

I wheeled on Fay and St. Onge. "Oh, I know," I went on in a mock singsong, "it's fashionable in some quarters"—here I shot a dark look around the room—

"it's fashionable, on the part of some, to say that corruption is a victimless offense, a victimless crime. After all, if there's a willing buyer and a willing seller, who gets hurt?

"I'll tell you who gets hurt, ladies and gentlemen. The mother who fears for her children's lives because there's faulty electric wiring in her housing project, since the inspector got paid off, that's who gets hurt. The parents whose kids buy drugs from a dope dealer who's on the street only because his case got fixed, that's who gets hurt. The taxpayers who are footing the bill because the contract didn't go to the low bidder, that's who gets hurt. Everybody who drinks the water in their own kitchen after the code officer is paid to look the other way, that's who gets hurt.

"And I'll tell you something else, ladies and gents. Those aren't the only victims of corruption. Corruption undermines the very institutions that we all count on to safeguard our liberties in this society. Nobody's going to want to hang on to a system where the perception is that the fix is in. Our democratic institutions—indeed, our elections themselves—are supposed to resolve competing claims for public dollars. If that system is undermined, if that system is rotten, then people are going to ask, what's the point? Why should I play by the rules?

"These are fundamental issues, my friends, and to belittle them by suggesting that public corruption is somehow a 'victimless crime' is an insult to every man and woman in this room." I stopped and took Napoleon's hand out of my suit.

Lanny gave a low whistle. "Like a duck to water," he said. "Either that or you've had a lot of practice in front of juries." I nodded.

"Now, what I want to know," Lanny added, "is can you teach it round or flat?"

"I can teach it round or flat," I said.

"Good," said Lanny. "We may need to."

Act One of the campaign for district attorney had just been played to completion, and not a word had been uttered in public. That's how I like it. That's how all serious litigators like it. Once you say anything in public, you diminish your flexibility.

For the next six months, I taught it pretty much flat out, six to twelve public appearances a day. You want to hear my stump speech? You just did.

Under the watchful eye of Lanny Green, we were careful not to oversell. I had been just an average assistant U.S. attorney in Brooklyn trying to do his job, we said, and we let the press discover—actually, Lanny made sure they discovered—that this average guy had gotten more than his share of scalps and ink. I was just a hardworking lawyer in an average firm, we said, though Lanny also made sure that a few columnists knew all about the illustrious history of Warfield & Coles, from helping to finance the mill towns of Massachusetts to taking a lead role in the civil rights movement—as well as the fact that I had made equity partner there in ten months, a record.

Nor, until the very end, did we come on too strong against Gross. If the message coming out of our campaign headquarters had been a sound, it would have been a sigh. This was in sorrow, not in anger. Lanny's posture was a shrug: a good man is trying to hang on too long; and young Terry Mullally here is the available man, in case you happen to agree with us that people shouldn't hang on too long.

I recognized this gambit immediately. It was the old Abe Fortas trick: define the issue so that you and the judge—in this case, the voter—are on one side, and everyone else is on the other side, especially opposing counsel or the opposing candidate. When Fortas was in private practice, he drove his adversaries crazy by persuading the judge that he wasn't an advocate for his client at all, he was just trying to help the court. The more his opponent protested, the more the opponent looked like a shrill partisan who couldn't be trusted to give the judge reliable information.

I knew Lanny wasn't a lawyer, so this maneuver didn't come from Abe Fortas. I said, "Everyone agrees people shouldn't hang on too long. How does that spell Mullally?"

"Because we say so," Lanny explained. "It comes from advertising. You draw a circle around one hundred percent of your market, with you on the inside and your competitors, especially the dreaded Brand X, on the outside. 'The closer you shave, the more you need Noxzema.' Everybody likes to think they shave close. 'Gleem, the toothpaste for people who can't brush after every meal.' Nobody brushes after every meal. Bingo, you have one hundred percent of the market, if they buy the assumption you smuggled into your slogan."

I laughed. "I was in Hong Kong on a case last year and my hotel bathroom had Hazeltine Snowbase creme, 'for delicate Asian skin.' Wonder what it would have been in Bratislava."

"For delicate Slovak skin," Lanny affirmed with no hesitation.

At the end of the day, though, the residue of Lanny's message was anything but cynical. His subtext, insistent and powerful even if delivered largely off-the-record behind closed doors and in whispers, was: Aren't we all lucky to have this fine Terry Mullally, this polished and accomplished lawyer and prosecutor, as the available man?

The only problem with our message was it was a lie.

chapter two

Why I Love Cops

My family would have laughed at the easy and super-confident image we projected for me throughout the 1996 campaign. If I had had any family.

My mother died giving life to me in November 1963. I'm named for my father. I'm Terrence Mullally, Jr.

My father was born in Dana, Massachusetts, the week of the big stock market crash in 1929. I was born the day the first Irish Catholic president got shot. Luck runs in the family.

When my father was eight, the whole town of Dana was flooded by the government to help create the Quabbin Reservoir in central Massachusetts. His world was wiped out. His family moved to Brooklyn, where his dad ran a jewelry store and his mom taught biology.

My father and I shared an apartment in South Brooklyn for the first five years of my life. The real estate agents renamed it Carroll Gardens in the seventies. Without my permission. I would still say I'm from

South Brooklyn, if anybody who knew the difference asked me.

There were crates of produce and hardware stacked in corners of the apartment at all times: flatirons, Frye boots, jellied cranberry sauce, you name it. I didn't wonder what my father did for a living. He was home a lot; that was good enough for me. I thought he might be a policeman, because he would frequently entertain men with blue uniforms. They moved crates of stuff around, and they would laugh a lot and drink beer. The men with blue uniforms would let me sit on their lap. They would let me play with the silver handcuffs on their belts, but they would not let me touch the leather holsters on their hips.

There were a few bushes and a tree in the parking lot outside our window, and my father and I spent a lot of time watching the birds, especially in winter. He would put me right up on the windowsill and hold me from behind, putting both arms around me tight. We watched the sparrows and the chickadees and the nuthatches and the slate-colored juncos. I told my father my favorites were the nuthatches, because they always walked upside down on the bark. My father called me his little nuthatch. He held me upside down by my ankles and tickled me, and I squealed. "That doesn't sound like a nuthatch!" he said, and I squealed some more.

When he wanted to get me to eat, he would pretend the spoon or fork was an airplane, sometimes the whole Irish Air Force, and it would zoom and vroom and dip and dive and climb and circle and buzz and somehow it always ended up right at the airplane hangar, which was my mouth, which opened just in time so the zooming buzzing airplane could go in. Even air transports and cargo planes carrying spinach in their hold landed safely in this manner.

My father was also an accomplished horse, and we were expert wrestlers. I remember him lying on his back on the floor in front of the fireplace and holding me on his chest, then gradually extending his arms while reciting a staccato narrative whose climax was that "Terry . . . is . . . FLYING!!" I remember squealing. I remember the warmth and smell of burning wood, and I remember what my father's aftershave smelled like then, too. Sometimes I would go bury my head in his pillow, and the smell was always there. I still use the same kind.

My father read to me often. Every night, I think. I remember liking a frog or a toad a lot, and being scared of a rat who was holding a rolling pin, to make a pie. I remember the words "Old Mother West Wind" and the words "The Merry Little Breezes." I remember a little otter being lost. I remember, I remember very clearly, my father saying the words, "Terry, you are such a big little nuthatch, tonight we'll read *Now We Are Six!*" I knew this meant I had been a good boy.

That's all I remember.

My father left me that afternoon. I understood he was going to the "where house." He never came back, never.

I was with Mrs. LoBello. She was reading to me. I

heard running on the stairs. I started to say, "No running on the stairs!" to make a joke. Three men with blue uniforms came in. They were not laughing or smiling. One of them spoke with Mrs. LoBello in the other room. She came back and picked me up. She was crying. The men were carrying crates around. "Don't worry, Terry, everything will be all right," said Mrs. LoBello. "Everything will be . . . just . . . fine!" She was crying a lot.

"Tough for the kid," I heard one of the men with a blue uniform say.

When I had nightmares, growing up, I would hear those words again and again, in a fugue state: tough for the kid tough for the kid tough for the kid tough for the kid tough.

I was almost five. I was told my father had died in an automobile accident. I was sent to a "group home"—what used to be called an orphanage. There were other kids. They were older than I was. I spent a lot of time by myself, a lot of time. I would go over in my head everything I could remember my father ever having said. I would say the words out loud. "Terry, are you all right?" the Sisters would ask from outside the door of my room. "Yes, I'm fine," I would say. "Just fine." I kept the door shut tight when I was in my room.

When I think of the group home today, what I remember most is being cold. It was always cold.

As I got a little older, seven and eight, I was frustrated that I couldn't remember more about my years with my father. Why hadn't I paid attention, so I could remember? I had just been enjoying myself, I had been heedless. I made up my mind I would always pay attention and remember, in case they came to take other things away from me, like my eyesight, or my sense of smell.

At least my father got to be eight before his world was ripped apart.

I was sent to parochial school, St. Agnes, where I was anxious to lose myself in my studies. The Sisters of Charity never had to tell *me* to pay attention, or to stop fidgeting. My favorite subjects were physics and Latin. I would do both of them endlessly in my head. Unlike the other kids, I loved memorizing the laws, memorizing the vocabulary. I was creating a structure that could not be taken away from me. The laws of physics and the rules of grammar were personal clubhouses for me. I would hide out in them. It was a play world, a real world, a world where I had equal footing. Superior footing, even.

"*Dic, duc, fer, fac,* remember this or get a whack." My knuckles were never rapped. Hail Mary, full of grace, blessed art thou among swimmers. Lessons learned for a lifetime.

At Christmas and Easter and Thanksgiving, for as long as I was at the group home, I refused to go spend the holiday with other kids and their aunts or uncles or cousins. I would stay at the group home. I told myself that some of the nuns were as lonesome as I was, though in retrospect I don't believe that was true. I also did not want the other kids to think I needed to sit by their relatives' hearth, or watch TV in their family room, whatever. Later, when I became a lawyer and a litigator and went into politics, nobody had to explain to me the meaning of the phrase "Never let them see you sweat."

In most matters, I have unusual powers of concentration and memory. I think they were the products of my terrible loneliness in the orphanage. I would read something once, even carelessly, and never forget it, not a word. I was practicing so that in case the warmth returned, I would be able to encapsulate it, to save it, to savor it.

"*Group* home." Hah! That was rich.

When I was in ninth grade, I was placed in a foster home in Brooklyn. The less said about that, the better.

I did have one relative, a cousin of my father's called Lonna, who still lived in New Salem, Massachusetts, right next to where Dana had been. She was a semi-invalid and couldn't take me in. I visited her in the summers, though, and I went fishing on the Quabbin Reservoir with her stepson. That beat the hell out of life in the foster home, I can tell you.

The transfer papers when they were sending me from the group home to the foster home listed my name as "Terrence NMI Mullally." NMI stood for No Middle Initial. That killed me. Like they were trying to rub it in. It might as well have said NR, No Relatives. And they forgot the "Jr."

*   *   *

The closest thing I had to family in Brooklyn was the neighborhood cops. They seemed to have an avuncular interest in me; they were as good friends as I had. There was a detective sergeant who everybody called Joe Balls—his real name was Joseph Ballaster—who used to take me places. He was a wonderful companion for a kid, a real father figure for me. He was a big, friendly black guy, all muscle, with a kind face, always a gentle expression. Thoughtful eyes.

Joe took me around Brighton Beach and Manhattan Beach. He took me fishing in Sheepshead Bay. We ate bluefish and mackerel at Gage & Tollner seafood, only three blocks from the orphanage.

On Sundays, we would walk over the bridge to Manhattan. I remember the smells of Yonah Schimmel's knishery and Kossar's Bialystoker Kuchen Bakery on the Lower East Side.

We went to the Fulton Fish Market, window-shopping with no windows. We ate at Carmine's Italian Seafood on Beekman and Angelo's on Mulberry Street in Little Italy. I couldn't believe people would let you sit at those beautiful huge oak tables whenever you wanted and bring you steaming hot plates of food. Joe introduced me to the people who ran Angelo's, and they were just as nice as he was.

I didn't mind letting Joe buy me things because he said he didn't really have a lot of family so I was doing him a favor by going walking with him on weekends. Later, I found out Joe had a wife, and two daughters who were younger than I was.

Joe took me to Chinese Park and Roosevelt Park in Chinatown. Or did I take him? Anyway, at the northern edge of Roosevelt Park, the old Chinese men would bring their songbirds out in the early morning to be warmed by the sun, so they would burst into song and sing to the old men the rest of the day. I thought if they had to do that, it must be gloomy inside where they lived. I didn't tell Joe that my father had called me his little nuthatch.

Sometimes we bought produce in Chinatown, on Pell Street, or Canal, or Mulberry. Chinese Park was at Bayard and Mulberry. Roosevelt Park was at Canal and Chrystie. I had the grid of every neighborhood in New York in my head. That came in handy later, when I worked dope and payoff cases on the street.

Finally, Joe took me uptown. We went to the Museum of Natural History. I loved the birds. I would squint so I couldn't see the guy wires. I wanted a peg leg like Peter Stuyvesant in the diorama.

We went fishing at Harlem Meer, at the northeast corner of Central Park. We went to the zoo. Joe bought me a cherry Coke in the Oak Room at the Plaza. It was dark and smelled good in there. I could have stayed for days.

"Look at those cliffs, Terry!" Joe said to me, hooking his thumb at the impassive walls of granite stretching up the other side of Fifth Avenue, well beyond my ability to crane my neck skyward. Ever since then, I've thought of Manhattan as cliffs and canyons, with all us bipeds perambulating through the canyons, liable to be ambushed from the second or third story of the cliff on either side at any moment. By a *Tyrannosaurus rex!*

As I got a few years older, Joe Balls took me to other parts of his beat as well: the Bowery, Eldridge and Houston, the meatpacking district in the West Village. He told me to stay away from Hangar Bar and Two Potato and a couple of other places, though he didn't say why. He took me inside a few bars, where everyone seemed to know him. Joe always had an easy manner with people.

We met other cops there, too, John Casey and Luis Garcia and Rudy Solano. Those three became my friends for life, but Joe Balls unaccountably dropped out of the picture when I was seventeen or so. It was as though he had given me a push, gotten me going on my way, and I just zoomed off into the rest of my life.

I didn't see Joe for a dozen years, but when I did, I'm proud to say I was able to serve the public interest and do him a good turn at the same time. That's my view, anyway; the U.S. attorney, John "Tarzan" Burroughs, saw it a little differently.

There were no girls at Bishop Ford High School— "Ford's" to the initiate—but there was an all-girls Jewish school a few blocks away. What a salad! Olive-skinned girls, big ancient-seeming eyes, vulnerable eyes. I hung around that school a lot. There was an abandoned warehouse near the fish market where I used to trespass after school, sometimes with a bunch of kids, sometimes with just one girl. I remember a girl named Tova. She was an unhappy person. She called me a "mackerel snatcher" because I ate fish on Fridays. I let this pass. I patted her knee. Then I patted it some more. Then we clawed at each other through our clothes. It made me feel warm, good. Her too, I think, but I didn't ask.

Eventually, I got to know the other kids at school better. I joined the chess club. We used to play chess outdoors a lot, at tables in Prospect Park. We could even play in our heads, without a board. I continued to read for hours on end: U.S. history, English literature, the classics. I had plenty of time for it. I remembered everything. When I was in eleventh grade the Franciscans told me I could get into Yale or Princeton, with my grades and aptitude scores.

This made me feel worse. I knew I wasn't going to Yale or Princeton. It just wasn't in my self-image— yet—and that was for social reasons, not intellectual ones. Looking back, I consider it nothing short of outrageous that imaginary social walls restrained me. This was a system failure, a market failure. I'd be even more bitter if the market failure hadn't occurred entirely within my own head. Something I read? Dickens, maybe. Certainly nothing the Sisters or the Franciscans had said.

I didn't have a penny, and I didn't have any relatives except Lonna, who was too sick to get down for my graduation. Nobody came to my graduation, except Casey and Garcia. I won the physics prize and the Latin prize and graduated fourth in my class of 280 kids. They made a big fuss over me, everybody clapped a lot. That made me feel better. It was the first time anyone had applauded for me. I enjoy applause. You actually get a lot of it in politics. It's a form of salary that taxpayers don't mind shelling out. So the Latin and physics prizes were in a way the kindling of political ambition in me.

I went to the Brooklyn College campus of the City University of New York, in Midwood. The open admissions policy I didn't need. Free I did need. I worked two jobs most semesters anyway. This left less time for girls than I would have liked, but I managed okay. I had absolutely no money for indulgences of any kind, but my studies seemed to take care of themselves. I graduated in 1984, and got into Fordham Law, which is a damn good school. Jesuit influence never hurt any institution I'm aware of.

I had one unusual extracurricular activity at CUNY: I was the only straight member of the Gay and Lesbian Society. I got along great with both the gays and the lesbos, even though they hated each other. I think the reason was, being an orphan—excuse me, a graduate of a "group home"—I sort of knew what it was like when people look crosswise at you, treat you funny. Or just not the same. I can't tell you how that enraged me. I had a history professor at CUNY who said the central theme of Western civilization, and particularly the American experience, was the idea that "the individual shall not be thrust in a corner." I loved that. I made up my mind no one was going to thrust me into a corner. I had spent enough time in the corner before I got to CUNY.

*   *   *

My other extracurricular activity was to get into
the deep country as often as I could. I had absorbed a
lot of Bible teachings from the sweet Sisters of
Charity, but I have always regarded the outdoors as
my cathedral. It started with fishing at Lonna's place
on the Quabbin. Fishing and hunting are a form of
communion for me. Blood of the Lamb, the Paschal
Lamb. Killing conquers death.

During my last two years at CUNY and all the way
through Fordham Law, I yearned for the world beyond
the cliffs: come Friday, I'd be dying to get out of town,
and get my toes into some dirt. You can fly a desk only
so long before you want to kill something or somebody. At least if you're me.

My entrée into this world was again my friends in
blue, whom I had met through Joe Balls. John Casey
was a patrolman, Luis Garcia a sergeant, and Rudy
Solano a detective sergeant when I first knew him, later
a detective lieutenant. These three introduced me to
the joys of hunting in Columbia County, N.Y., just two
hours north of the City. Deer and turkey, both good
for the patience and the concentration required of a
trial lawyer. There was plenty of sparsely posted land
there, so you could hunt almost legally. Casey owned a
falling-down ramshackle barn, covered with honey-
suckle, just off Route 22 in Austerlitz. We called it
Mudville, and used it as a base of operations.

I have never slept in such squalor, nor enjoyed
myself more. There was an old Dandy stove in one corner of the main room, and we always cooked the same
thing: spaghetti and meatballs straight from the can.

The side course was exchanging sophomoric tips on the stock market. There were four crude bunks, and a trunk full of sleeping bags and blankets that the locals seemed to know better than to steal. The wind whipped through the slats of that barn at night, but we didn't mind. "If it's brown, it's down" was the camp motto, and this applied to both deer and whiskey.

One time, a brief fling of mine at law school learned I was going to be north for the weekend and tactfully invited herself. "It's guys only," I said. "Raunchy scene. I mean, you're welcome to come on the trip, but you run the risk of being passed around like a ham sandwich—who needs that?"

Her hand shot up in the air. "I do!" My shoulders slumped. "Just a little nibble at a time," she added, whether by way of warning or guidance.

I demurred, and no ladies ever darkened the door of Casey's barn. I suspect everybody was the better for it.

I began shooting tin cans, first with a .22 and then with a Savage .308 that belonged to Solano. When I was twenty, Casey and Garcia chipped in to buy me a matching .308 of my own, which has served me well and which I still possess, though I do not get out as much as I used to. We shot tin cans and beer bottles well after dusk, using infrared scopes—just to "sight in" the guns before the next day's shoot, you understand. Not to be confused with it also being endlessly enjoyable. The unluckiest thing you could be at that camp was a used can of Chef Boyardee after dark.

Throughout my twenties, hunting was not only a great release for me, but also a way to keep close with

my friends in blue. We preferred to hunt in nasty
woods rather than in open areas where we might
encounter other hunters. The weather in that part of
New York State in late winter is so changeable that on
the same day you're likely to find several feet of snow
next to roads made impassable by mud. I remember
bringing hip boots and snowshoes to Casey's barn and
needing to use them both within an hour.

Casey and Garcia were relatively lazy hunters, in
my view. They'd go out at daylight. Solano and I both
liked to get out a couple of hours before dawn, to wake
up with the woods. You're more a part of the woods if
you've woken up in them and with them. That's
important. In politics, you want to be at one with the
people; in hunting, you want to be at one with the
woods.

We usually still-hunted: take three steps, then stop
and listen. One thing old Tarzan taught me is that in
litigation, nine times out of ten the best thing to do is
nothing. Same in deer hunting: nine times out of ten
the best thing to do is wait.

The cops said I had unusual calm for a young
hunter. Especially one from Brooklyn. Guys from
Brooklyn are famous for getting buck fever, shooting
cows. Not too many deer in Brooklyn, I guess. Or cows.

As with any activity that becomes a major part of
your life, you tend to remember the first time with special clarity. Mine was mid-November, thick carpet of
leaves on the ground. It had poured rain for two days, so
the woods were quiet. A few hundred yards uphill from
the barn there was an apple orchard, where Solano and

I had made cider in Casey's old barrel grinder on a Friday afternoon. We dumped the pomace—the apple pulp—deep in a thick spruce cover farther up the hill.

That evening, we all enjoyed the cider with our spaghetti and meatballs. Rudy and I saw no need to mention the pomace. We volunteered to tackle the thick uphill cover on the next morning's drive. Casey and Garcia were delighted to take the easier oak and maple territory that fell gradually downhill to the stream.

In the morning, Rudy took the left, I took the right, and we agreed to converge in half a mile. In hunting, you get out what you put in, so I made for the heaviest brambles and nastiest spruce and cedar. I was losing my orange wool cap to a spiked branch with every step, so with some irritation, I shoved it in my pocket. I was pretty sure Rudy would never take a brush shot.

I came to a clearing—buckwheat and millet, white birches to the right, another spruce cover fifty yards in front of me—and stopped at the edge. I opened my mouth as wide as I could, to show no breath and cut the sound of breathing. It was still so early the birches looked yellow. Your eyes play tricks on you before dawn and at twilight, between dog and wolf.

I heard a stick snap and pushed the safety off, moving nothing but my thumb. Another twig snapped, then another. The head of a big doe appeared above some cedars, then sank, then appeared again ten yards away, as though in a Punch-and-Judy show. She was going full tilt.

When she emerged from the cedars, she kept on a dead run but seemed to shrink to half her former height. No more jumping: instinctively she knew that in the open, the lowest profile was the best.

Then she jumped again, straight up, and plunged forward in a beautiful, agonizing slow-motion spiral. I was aware I was running toward the deer. Stay down, I commanded. Please stay down, I pleaded. I felt light-headed. Rudy was already standing over the deer as I pulled up.

"Nice shot, kid," he said.

"Was that mine?" I only then realized I had fired. "Did you shoot?"

"No, kid, that was all yours. If I had fired, you would've heard it. You don't hear your own shot, because the adrenaline is carrying you, you're concentrating a hundred percent on the animal. It's like, you're nervous at every wedding but your own, you know?" He chuckled and rolled the deer's head to one side with his boot.

"You caught her right under the shoulder, beautiful." Mindful of the Mudville motto, Rudy drew a pint of whiskey from his pocket and had a stiff belt off the neck.

Over time, I must have dropped ten animals in a row before I finally missed, in my sixth or seventh year hunting, on a passing shot. In thinking about it, I guess passing shots are okay in duck hunting—you don't have much choice with pintail, for example, or teal or wood duck—but I don't think they're advisable in deer hunting. If you were going to make a mistake, that's probably how it would happen. And just as a partridge doesn't fly very far, deer won't really run very far, usually no more than half a mile if you haven't fired. Think of that as eight hundred yards. If you are patient, and take a few steps at a time and then listen, you can often get closer than a hundred yards to a deer. At that range, especially if you have a good scope, the gun does everything but field-dress the animal.

We also used to go duck hunting on the Great South Bay, getting up at oh-dark-hundred and driving east. Our quarry was the ocean ducks: broadbill, scaup, blue- and green-wing teal, and the Canadian yellowlegs, the tastiest and largest form of black duck. This was right on the flyway. Garcia kept a Barnegat Bay "scooter," a low-slung craft with a single set of oars, anchored to a cement block in the reeds. We carried it to the water, and it was truly heavier than a dead minister, as Luis advertised. The ride on the ocean swell was somewhat alarming, as we were dressed in thick woolens and there were only six inches of freeboard. All of us knew a cop who had drowned in a storm off Rowayton, Connecticut, in one of these babies. Wife and four kids, and it had to be him.

The scooter served its purpose, because when you ducked your head into the hull, no threatening profile was presented to a squadron of incoming broadbill. If it looked as though the ducks were going to blow by at seventy miles an hour, as it often did, you would raise one arm out of the hold and wave a blue or red handkerchief, then quickly withdraw it. This apparently had a "whazzat?!" effect on the ducks, who could not believe what they had seen or not seen and who would regularly peel back around to investigate. Easy shot, the second time by.

Sometimes we would put into shore and tramp the marshes, looking to put up a black duck or Canada goose from the irrigation ditches they call dreens. Casey and Solano both had their noses straight up in the air as far as the Canada geese were concerned, calling them "sky carp," as they were known in Columbia County, where they fouled farms and golf courses by the hundreds. But if one of them got up out of a ditch ten feet in front of you, it was like a B-52 bomber taking off. And being able to bring down a B-52 with a 12-gauge was a trip.

I didn't own a shotgun, so they let me shoot a Churchill side-by-side the cops had confiscated from some dope dealer. I don't know what he was doing with that object of beauty. Talk about pearls before swine!

During Fordham Law I interned at the Brooklyn U.S. attorney's office, and when I graduated, my pals who wore blue during the week and full camo on weekends helped get me a permanent job there. They didn't write letters, either, as you would to get somebody into a Wall Street firm. Anyone who's ever been a prosecutor or a defense lawyer, or a cop or a crook, knows you never write when you can call, and never call when you can nod. Ambiguously. Saves time, maintains your options. On occasion it can even prevent bad things from happening.

On June 21, 1987, after two weeks in the upstate woods to get some fresh air into my lungs, I reported for duty as an assistant United States attorney for the Eastern District of New York. I thought I would stay for three years, get the jury trial experience, and then move to a big firm to make money, as I was sick to death of not having two nickels to rub together. I wound up staying seven and a half years in that office, and would have stayed longer if I hadn't been forced out. Too bad. I could've been a great DA in Brooklyn.

That was my plan, anyway; but as the man says, you never know where your next coalition is coming from. Or where it's going to take you. That's the great thing about coalitions. They've got about as much directional sense as a school of minnows.

chapter three

A Beacon Hill Dinner Party

The move from New York prosecuting to Boston private law practice was like shifting from fourth gear to second at sixty miles an hour. The billing power of Warfield & Coles rested less on its size than its social connections. I met a couple of smoothies, to be sure, but I also ran into a good number of wellborn idiots. I began to worry that I had landed in a backwater, and a tepid one at that. On slow days, I worried about getting the bends.

My doubts about Boston's social possibilities were confirmed and erased on the same evening in March of 1996. The young probate attorney with the office next to mine, one Herman Pennyfeather, confided that the Truslows were short a male human being for a small dinner at their Louisburg Square town house that Friday, and would I care to leap into the breach?

I would and I did.

Herman asked if he could swing by my place after work and pick me up on the way to the party. I laughed out loud at the thought of a sixteenth-generation Harvard-trained Pennyfeather trying to find Oak Square in Brighton in his BMW.

"What's funny?"

"Oh nothing. I've just got so much work to do I couldn't dream of going home first. I'll have to walk up from here." Herman reluctantly agreed to join me on foot for the arduous six-block march up State, Tremont, and Beacon. On the way, I rather crudely asked about the guest list.

"This is a good invitation for you, Terry. These are definitely *not* the beautiful people of whom I know you are so well enamored."

Herman was aware from our brown bag lunches what I professed to think about people who look for themselves in the society pages. I said, "How so?"

"Your beautiful people may hail from Weston, or Dover, or Sherborn, and they are Very Important and Captains of Finance, and Trustees of this and that. These here tonight are basically North Shore people, serious drinkers—not so easy to find nowadays—most of them with places in town, too, and the wonderful thing about them is they *know* they're no damn good."

My opinion of Herman Pennyfeather, whom I had contemned because of his name and his specializing in wills and trusts, was rising: at least he seemed to have a bad word for everybody.

The walk is straight uphill until you get to the crest of Mount Vernon Street, and we arrived somewhat sweaty at the town house. Our host and hostess greeted us amiably on the front steps, where they were standing with drinks in their hands and chatting in high voices to each other as though they had just met. In fact, they had been married for thirty years. It became apparent they were talking about the guests who had entered the house immediately ahead of us. I wondered how Herman and I, the Odd Couple if ever there was one, would fare. But once we pushed into the first-floor living room, I forgot the troubles and uncertainties of our voyage.

People say that at a typical New York–Boston wedding, you can dress two hundred Bostonians off the backs of three of the New Yorkers. You couldn't prove it by this lot. Sitting around on the most handsome furniture I've ever seen was a set of sculpted figures of women, living figurines. Features, hair, dresses, ankles, and shoes all carved. They were caryatids, holding up a world I wanted to inhabit.

"Well, if it isn't the Gibson Girls," I blurted.

"Forgive him, he's a blow-in," Herman said.

"Herman, where have you found this object of innocence? Is he our Missing Link?"

I stuck out my hand. "Terry Mullally, ma'am, working at Warfield & Coles, wage slave, just moved from Boston South, that is, New York City."

"I seeeeee. Ruthie, get over quick! We've got a live one here: an honest-to-goodness red-blooded two-toilet lace-curtain Irishman in our midst! Just the thing to thicken the old stock." She turned her head partly back in my direction, but did not face me. "We're trying to marry off Ruthie," she added rather absentmindedly.

"Thanks *sooo* much for the introduction, Auntie

Vye," Ruthie gushed. "Could I get you anything to drink, Mr. Mullally?"

"Glass of white be lovely."

"Regrettably all we have is hard liquor."

I was floored. And it was true. I settled for I. W. Harper straight up. It occupied the bottom quarter of a Budweiser mug. "Awfully sorry," said Ruthie. "Beer tastes and a champagne pocketbook. *Such* a burden."

I sat down next to a highly polished cherrywood gun chest, inlaid with brass, which had been set on teak legs to form a coffee table. There were enormous tea caddy lamps to either side, and a single volume tossed off-center on the chest: a well-thumbed copy of Walter Muir Whitehill's *Topographical History of Boston*. It was not there for display.

The conversation seemed to be a series of sculpted pieces no less than the occupants of the furniture.

"Auntie, tell us about your trip."

"Well, my dears. I've just been to Africa all summer on safari, and I must say it made me *proud* of my Puritan blood. I mean, our people came here and they cut down the trees and killed the Indians and really made something of a go of it. Those people, those *Africans*"—here she sputtered to a dead halt, then collected herself for another run at her topic—"I mean, they've been there for *thousands* of years, and they don't even have *air-conditioning*."

Nobody missed a beat. "Auntie, tell Mr. Maloney how you deal with rising food prices."

"Rising food prices? I can never understand what they're *talking about* in the newspapers. I mean, you just take *more money* to the *grocery* store." Some laughter, lower this time. The collective attention was moving on.

"But, darlings, isn't that right?" Auntie Vye's protest was faint. She knew better than to force a losing hand.

They were indeed trying to marry off Ruthie. At dinner, Herman was seated to her right and I to her left. I fully expected huge butterfly pins to shoot out from the pantry to secure us in our places, and thus preserve us as specimens. To my left was a tall and rather disorganized-looking twenty-something woman with dirty blond hair. She had a wan air, and for some reason I took her to be someone who had recently suffered either a reversal in love or a death in the family. I turned to Ruthie: "I understand all people talk about in Boston is politics, sports, and revenge."

"Oh, no," said Ruthie. "That's what the stupid people who run the place talk about. We're the do-nothings who only used to own the place. So what we talk about is the stuff in Ralph Lauren ads at the front of the *New York Times* Sunday magazine section."

"The clothes?"

"No, silly. Those ads aren't about clothes. They're about money, and sex, and leisure time, oodles and oodles of leisure time. Not necessarily in that order."

She, for one, was as good as her word. It emerged that Ruthie had studied anthropology at a junior college on the North Shore, and was not unfamiliar with the propensity of various ages of humankind, and various tribes, to "do it" either missionary- or doggiestyle. Her knowledge was shared all around.

Following this clinical romp through the ages, Ruthie led us in a game of Politically Correct, offering the first entry herself: "The male sex drive involves no element of desire for dominion over the female." Murmurs of appreciation.

Whereupon the lady to my left played a trump: "No, no: 'There is no such thing as the male sex drive.'"

"Excellent!" piped a mannered male voice from the doorway. Two wavy-haired young men in black tie had joined us. They wore gold medallions around their necks, one with a yellow ribbon and one with a green.

"Terry, I want you to meet Roger Pingeon, a *great* friend of mine," Ruthie quickly put in.

"It's a pleasure," I said warmly.

"The pleasure is mine. This is my friend Niccolò."

"Where are you all from?" I inquired.

"Oh, my accent?" said Roger. "It's pure affectation."

Niccolò was equal to the task of carrying on the previous motif. "I can't understand why a woman could ever be unhappy," he whispered to us conspiratorially. "She carries around with her at all times the greatest thing in the world."

Roger was quick: "For that matter, Nick, you've been sitting on a gold mine your entire life."

There was an intake of breath around our end of the table, and the new arrivals sat down to join us. To their credit, they did not seem self-conscious about their precious cargo.

"What's the significance of the different-colored ribbons?" I asked Roger, to change the subject.

"We're on our way over to the Somerset for a club

dinner, *medallions to be worn*, and the color of the ribbon matches the decade you or your family joined the club. Nick's is seventies, mine is forties."

"Roger, I think you must be mistaken," said Auntie Vye with some concern. "My Buster joined the Somerset when he got back from the War, and I'm quite certain his ribbon was red, not green."

"Dear lady," Roger explained mildly, "I didn't mean to suggest we joined in the *nineteen*-forties."

This seemed to satisfy Auntie Vye. Roger, though, thought he had dealt too straight a blow, and made haste to cushion it.

"You really should have seen Buster tread the boards, Mr. Mullally," he declared, "especially in the musicals. He had the most fabulous ear for melody; so much so, he once told me he couldn't readily distinguish between people talking and singing." There was a small silence.

"My Buster retired early," said Auntie Vye dully, and whether or not it was her intention, I could see this made Roger feel even worse.

Dinner was beef Stroganoff and fresh asparagus, cooked and served by Ruthie herself. I counted it as a plus that a family who obviously could afford domestic help didn't have any. Ruthie issued ritual apologies for the meager fare, and received a backhanded compliment from Auntie Vye: "My dear, it's not what's on the *table* that's important, it's what's on the *chairs*." I shifted uneasily in mine, and turned to the dinner partner I had ignored on my left.

"How do you keep body and soul together?" I began.

The sun came out. The sad air was routed by an incandescent smile. A warming smile. "Oh, I'm a poor wage slave like yourself, at Rankin and Shaw on Congress Street. Real estate law. Emma Gallaudette," she said while offering her hand confidently. I realized I had not even introduced myself, but it seemed all right. Everything seemed all right. I shook her hand, mumbling my name.

"I know, I know. I heard your life history on your entrance—at least as summarized by you and Auntie Vye. Are you Catholic? I am."

I admired her skill at putting an outlander at ease. She obviously understood that the boldest conversational gambit is often the most polite: it sets interlocutors in common cause.

"Is this your circle?" I asked.

"Lord, no. I mean, I love Ruthie, but I don't really have any friends, much less a circle. My best friends growing up in Wellesley were always birds and fish."

I found the self-deprecation welcome, if hard to believe. The more she talked herself down—and she continued in this vein for some time—the more her smile and her voice gave promise of rooms lined with mahogany so old it's black as teak, of glassware so old it's wavy, of liqueurs so old they all taste like peach nectar. Boston has acres of that stuff, much more so than even Manhattan, let alone Brooklyn, and I confess I was well pleased to have landed in the middle of it. From my ravenous readings at Ford's, through college and law school, I had developed champagne tastes to go with my small-beer pocketbook. Pity that champagne and beer don't mix. Except, apparently, in Louisburg Square.

By way of comment on the companions of her youth, I explained my fondness for the outdoors, and touched lightly on my connection with the Quabbin Reservoir through my father. My *late* father, I said, in a quick, bright self-assured tone that meant there are no problems here at all, just don't ask any questions. Not now.

Emma dipped one eyebrow at the mention of my late father to show she understood perfectly, then used the same cheerful but banked tone to introduce gently a topic that otherwise could have sent my mouthful of Stroganoff onto the table.

"Oh, how *lovely*," she said, touching my arm lightly. "You and I are just the same, then." I felt warm. "I wish," she went on, "I wish my *husband* enjoyed the outdoors more. All he seems to care about is business." I felt a chill. A shudder, really.

Never let 'em see you sweat. "Oh, what's his line of business?"—my nonchalant tone suggesting I had been happily awaiting the arrival of a spouse into our conversation.

"He used to be an academic, international business law. That's where I met him, when I was at law school and he was a visiting professor."

"Did you go to Harvard Law?"

"No, I guess I wasn't sure I'd make the grade, so I went to Yale."

I happened to know that Yale Law was six times as hard to get into as Harvard Law, but I let this pass.

"Anyway, he's given up the academic stuff and travels a lot on business now, mainly the Far East. He's from Taiwan, and spends a ton of time in Hong Kong. With the handover to the Mainland Chinese coming up, there's a lot of money changing hands, a lot of money being made. Technically, it's mergers and acquisitions and public offerings—particularly the 'red chips,' the companies based on the mainland—but people are so manic about everything because of the politics in the background, the movement on the Hong Kong exchange is more technical than fundamental. It's almost like arbitrage. So Elijah has to be there. But do you know Plum Island, off Newburyport? If you're a serious birder at all, it's the best Massachusetts has to offer. My family used to have a cottage there."

So she could go from zero to brilliant in two seconds, and then back to zero. No, I didn't know Plum Island. I would very much like to know Plum Island, to see the birds, the birds at Plum Island. I was desperately repeating myself to prolong the conversation. Did she—

"Time for an ADD!" someone yelled, and the party repaired to the living room. On the way in, Emma touched my arm again and explained this was the acronym for an after-dinner drink. My elbow felt hot. She suggested we link arms and drink a Roman toast— each drinks from his or her own cup—from the silver goblets of stingers being passed around on salvers. It seemed such a good idea we executed the maneuver twice. My arm was on fire. I asked Emma rather stupidly if she would show me the birds on Plum Island some time. Now it was Auntie Vye who interrupted us:

"Tell me honestly, Mr. Malloy, what's your governing passion in life?"

"My governing passion is to have no passion."

"I don't believe you for a minute. Your cheeks are flushed. Anyway, *my* governing passion, since you ask, is fear of boredom."

She lowered her voice, took me to one side, and pressed my hand. "If Ruthie for any reason isn't your type, dear boy, there's always Alice Tippingham. She's *actually* got quite a good figure!" exclaimed Auntie Vye in surprise and delight. Then her voice trailed off. "Of course, I don't think she uses it much . . ." Pause. "She should have been here, but she was doing *good works* or some damn thing. *Finding* herself, perhaps." Auntie Vye smiled brightly. So did I. Ruthie? Alice? Not bloody likely.

I did remember to thank Ruthie and the senior Truslows. "Nice family," I said to Herman when we got out onto the cobblestones. But I wasn't thinking of the Truslows, to tell you the truth. I now knew, I knew to a certainty, what I had to have.

"What's the matter with you?" Herman's cheeks rose to his eyes in an expression of concern. "You look like you got hit with a stick."

"It's nothing," I said. "I just remembered I may have left my coffee machine on at home this morning. Hate to burn down Oak Square. Historic neighborhood."

"Yeh." Herman looked at me. He put a hand on my shoulder. "Do yourself a favor, pal. Stay away from those killer coffee machines. They'll getcha every time."

chapter four

A Breakfast in South Boston

When it rains, it pours. Less than a week after my introduction to Louisburg Square, they fired the starter's pistol for the district attorney's race. I felt like a dog that has finally caught a moving car and chomped down on the rear bumper. Be careful what you wish for.

The unofficial kickoff was the brunch hosted by State Senator William "Sonny" O'Reilly at the Easter Rising on Farragut Street in South Boston on March 17, St. Patrick's Day. Excuse me, Evacuation Day! The British left town, so the town gets stinko. It's the same straight logical path as everything else in Boston politics. Just as straight as Tremont Street. Ask any native.

Everybody who is anybody in the city, plus all wanna-bes, forgathers every year at the James Michael Curley Center in the L Street Bathhouse at around 9:00 A.M. to stagger up the hill to the Easter Rising. It is entirely fitting that this career-making, career-breaking day should begin under the watchful eye of Curley, the legendary bad boy who served two terms in prison and along the way was elected mayor of the city of Boston four times—each one in a different decade. That would have made for quite a chestful of ribbons at the Somerset Club! But I doubt he ever passed that particular threshold.

Curley lost as often as he won, and "inexplicably" amassed a fortune while in office. I wasn't quite sure how much I begrudged him that, though, because he was an authentic man of the people. He was also a master of the King's English, and as close as I had to a political hero. I felt that if I kept his example in mind, I might actually enjoy the game of politics.

For those in the know, there is an amply stocked bar in the basement of the Easter Rising, where many hang out until Senator O'Reilly and his party make the scene. Special guests come in via the world's most rickety fire escape on the second floor. According to posted signs, the state fire marshal has pegged the capacity of the joint at three hundred; on this occasion, it holds over seven hundred every year, and no one has ever been heard to complain. Or at least complain and live. There is grease everywhere, old oak and cheap pine everywhere, nothing but old oak and pine. One match, make the Cocoanut Grove fire look like a summer cookout.

The proceedings always start off with a number of Irish songs to make the heathen feel uncomfortable. "The Wild Colonial Boy" is a staple, as are "The Bold O'Donoghue," "Four Green Fields," "Galway Bay," "The Minstrel Boy," "The Wearin' o' the Green," "O'Brien Had No Place to Go," and, of course, "The Soldier's Song," the anthem of Ireland.

There are twenty or twenty-five speakers every year, right down to the bit players, anybody running for anything and any major player even thinking about running for something, including reelection. Most of the younger guys and gals are scared stiff; they take the mike upon invitation from O'Reilly, stand in one place like a statue, and fire off all their lines quick before they forget them. Or at least that's how it looked to me. There is a standing mike, no podium, so nobody can read from cards. This is not by accident. The standing mike is, in fact, brilliantly designed to keep Republican candidates from coming. Republicans always need cue cards, it's genetic or something.

You look like an idiot if you read from cue cards at a standing mike. Being able to talk for ten or fifteen minutes without notes is an absolute requirement of passage in Democratic politics in Massachusetts—one I had fortunately satisfied, thanks to our nation's jury system, before I arrived in the state.

For the 1996 event, I got there early, wolfed down my corned beef, cabbage, potatoes, and turnips, and noticed that the water glasses of the prominent state legislators seated on either side of me on the dais smelled a lot like gin. I was delighted to note also the absence of District Attorney Martin Gross.

First up was O'Reilly. He seemed to live with no other thought than to needle our Yankee Republican governor, Archibald Lovett, a/k/a "Mister Magoo," who actually attended this event wearing a bow tie. "Isn't he a good sport?" O'Reilly would inquire, meaning, "Isn't he a loser!" The governor grinned sheepishly, as usual.

Lovett in all candor was not a favorite of mine, though he had high approval ratings with the public at large. In a campaign for Congress early in his career, in a safe Republican district, he had publicly referred to his opponent as "a well-balanced Irishman, with a big chip on each shoulder." I never forgot that, and I never forgave Lovett. That remark is only a hop, skip, and a jump from "Hit him again, he's Irish!" I didn't need Whitehill's *Topographical History* to tell me those words had echoed along Boston's wharves for a century.

Since his first couple of runs, Lovett had successfully assumed an air of bewildered amiability. His unvarying expression was that of a man who had no idea what garden of earthly delights must surely await him just around the next turn in the road. I felt certain this was a mask. Lovett's family had made a fortune in plate glass and hides, though they had not been "in trade" for over a hundred years. He clearly enjoyed the finer things in life. He must, I thought, despise the grasping office seekers who were his daily companions.

Worse, from my point of view, Lovett's standoffish manner had somehow enabled him to acquire a reputation for shyness. Remembering his gibe at my people, I found this galling. Shy my eye. More like one part shy and nine parts screw you.

So I was tickled by O'Reilly's initial salvo: "Behold our governor! To a battle of wits, he comes unarmed!" This was not even "A-roll" material, but the water of life had begun to work its magic even at that hour, and the place erupted.

"Fellow designated drivers!" O'Reilly went on. Much

mirth. "The governor has a new proposal to crack down on drunk driving by reducing the forbidden blood alcohol content to point-oh-eight." He wheeled on Lovett. "Governor, some of our people were *born* at point-oh-eight!" Convulsions.

"Now don't be being too hard on the governor," he solemnly advised the crowd. "He and his ilk have been more than kind to us Hibernians these last several hundreds of years." He turned to Lovett again. "And we do want to thank you for letting us use your country!" Crowd helpless.

"With abundant gratitude to Hal Roach, Ireland's great international comedian, I have a parchment I should like to read in your honor, Your Excellency," O'Reilly went on, unfurling a scroll:

"The Governor is my shepherd, I'm in want.
He maketh me to lie down on park benches.
He leadeth me beside the still factories,
He disturbeth my soul.
Yea, though I walk through the valley of the
    shadow of Depression and Recession,
I anticipate no recovery, for He is with me.
He prepareth a reduction in my salary in the
    presence of my enemies,
He anointeth my small income with great
    losses,
My expense runneth over.
Surely unemployment and poverty shall fol-
    low me all the days of my life,
And I shall dwell in a mortgaged house forever."

O'Reilly hurried on. "What a place! And it's great to see the mayor here! As I was walking in, I heard a fellow telling his buddy that his brother worked hard on the mayor's campaign in hopes of getting a job with the city. 'What's he doing now?' the buddy asked. 'Nothing. He got the job!'"

The mayor was not amused.

"And it's great to see the *lieutenant* governor, too," O'Reilly went on, hitting the adjective so hard everyone forgot this was the second-ranking office in all of state government. "I saw him greet a voter at the door, and he said, 'How do you do? I'm the lieutenant governor.' And the fellow said, 'Well, nice to meet you. What do you do?' And the lieutenant governor replied, 'I just did it.'"

To show he meant no harm, O'Reilly put a hand on the lieutenant governor's shoulder and asked him innocently, "Why do they call you Lite Guv, anyway? Or is it Guv Lite? Which is it?"

Let me phrase the question, I thought to myself, and it doesn't matter how you answer.

I regret having to report that the "clueless" Governor Lovett gave almost as good as he got. The first words out of his mouth were, "Senator, it is I who am indebted to you. Thank *you* for letting us use your *State House*, these past five years!" It was a sore point among the city's Irish Democrat elite that they had let the governorship fall into unfamiliar hands two terms in a row. They had at least three more years of bow ties to endure at the Feast of the Saint. Lovett cheerfully rubbed their noses in that fact. He beamed at O'Reilly and with both hands straightened his bow tie, which did not need straightening.

Lovett was well known for telling audiences that his ancestors had arrived in Plymouth, Mass., in 1630 with nothing but the shirts on their backs and eight thousand pounds of gold. He steadfastly denied that his family had come over on the *Mayflower*, insisting that they had sent the servants over on that barque to get the summer cottage ready against their arrival.

Rather than repeat the *Mayflower* bit this year, Mister Magoo launched into a fetching shaggy dog story. In a doleful voice:

"Many years ago, a young boy from potato country set out on an ocean voyage for a strange land. When he arrived, he was taken to live in brick tenement buildings among his relatives and close countrymen. Upon leaving school, he found many doors shut to him in his desired profession; there was a rigid class system at work. So he found employment with relatives, and made a name for himself. After much travail, he was finally accepted among the councils of the ruling elite in their chosen pursuits."

Every Irishman in the audience could identify with that, and a few muttered sympathetically. But suddenly Lovett's voice and demeanor changed, becoming full of good cheer and confidence.

"Ladies and gentlemen, this poor young fellow was *myself*. The potato country was not Ireland but Eastern Long Island, New York. The boat was the Port Jefferson Ferry. I landed at Boston and was housed in a brick tenement-style dormitory at *prep school* with my cousins the Saltonstalls, the Lees, and the Lowells. I wanted to go into politics but the way was blocked.

So I joined my Yankee cousins on the boards of half a dozen banks and insurance companies. As you know, I overcame adversity and did well enough financially. But the true sign of my admission to the councils of the ruling elite is your invitation, Senator O'Reilly, to join you all here at these proceedings this very day!"

This actually engendered a certain amount of foot stomping for our reputedly dour and desiccated governor.

"People say I have a love/hate relationship with Senator O'Reilly," Lovett continued. "It is not true. I greatly admire a man who, by his own admission— nay, his own boast—can slap a tax on a galloping horse!" Lovett was death on taxes, so this sold.

"Candidly, some of my political advisers said I should not be here this morning," he plunged on. "But I want you to know that I do not shun controversy. I will take a stand on any issue at any time, and many are wondering what I truly feel about William 'Sonny' O'Reilly.

"If, when you say 'Sonny O'Reilly,' you mean the sultan of South Boston, the suzerain of the State House, the tyrant who terrorizes the goo-goos and suckles the suspect; the dictatorial oppressor whose fast gavel denies every citizen a vote on term limits; if you mean the evil man behind the hateful Democratic machine, the kingmaker who ignores the public will; the crony *di tutti* cronies; the power broker of patronage at the Massachusetts Bay Transportation Authority; if you mean the very man who thwarts everything that is good and right and pure about Massachusetts—then certainly I am against him.

"But if, when you say 'Sonny O'Reilly,' you mean the learned leader of his esteemed Chamber; the sage whose single word steers his colleagues back from the wayward path; the saint of East First Street; the pious husband of Jennie and loving father of the O'Reilly brood; if you mean the champion of the working man and the guardian of the widowed; the trustee of The Hospital and the patron of The Library; the man who would open our Commonwealth's beaches to all and extend to every child, rich or poor, the opportunity to attend the school of his or her choice—then certainly I am for him.

"That is my stand. I will not retreat from it. I will not compromise."

I was beginning to see how Lovett could get elected in Massachusetts despite wearing a bow tie. That didn't mean I had to like it, though.

O'Reilly gave me the mike about 11:30 A.M. I knew I had to do some high stepping, but I was prepared. I went right at him.

"Senator O'Reilly, it's great to be in your bailiwick. South Boston is such an old-fashioned place. One of the country's last true, old-style ward bosses operates here. He has five hundred registered Democrats under- neath him." Pause. "He cuts the grass at St. Augustine's Cemetery." This was received mezzo mezzo.

"Actually, Senator, I've heard that some of the res- idents of St. Augustine's are up in arms, what with this talk of you potentially leaving office in a few years. A couple of them said that if they can't vote for Sonny O'Reilly, they might as well *stay* dead.

"I understand that Senator O'Reilly has recently

said he may come out in favor of term limits. That's kind of like Caligula, late in life, endorsing celibacy." Crowd warming up a little. A few people actually stopped shoveling food into their mouths and looked up at me. But I noticed they were still chewing.

Out of the corner of my eye I espied the extremely handsome state senator from Revere and Chelsea trying to elbow his way through the crowd toward the dais. This guy was a big-time supporter of Martin Gross and would be in his corner all the way. I therefore put the spotlight on him, placed him right in the crosshairs to freeze his advance in an awkward position. "Ah, but it's good to see Senator Reinhardt here!" I exclaimed. "Always a pleasure, Senator. And, tell us, how are things in Chelsea, under the bridge? Not so good, I hear. In fact, ladies and gentlemen, I have heard times are so tough in Chelsea that the local influence peddlers have had to lay off several city councillors!"

Southie loved this; Southie was accustomed to having everybody else step on its fingers on the lower rungs of the ladder, and Chelsea was definitely down there on a rung below Southie. Three of the sitting city councillors in Chelsea in fact had seen the inside of the Big House.

"Senator, I was surprised to hear that your leading candidate for mayor in Chelsea has said if he is elected and gets to preside over the city and its bustling business establishment, he will serve only one term."

"That's right," shot back Senator Reinhardt, assuming a jaunty air. He probably practiced with an FDR-style cigarette holder in the privacy of his office.

"But, Senator," I returned. "I would have thought that would be up to the sentencing judge."

This was deemed by most to have crossed the line, but I could see that O'Reilly, at least, was amused, and he was my major quarry. I decided to flatter him by insulting him.

"Say, Senator O'Reilly, I have a question for all the members of the press who are here." O'Reilly was well known for despising the press, and the favor was returned. "Did all you Solons of the Fourth Estate hear about the big lunch the other day? The good Sonny O'Reilly, the nefarious Sonny O'Reilly, the Easter Bunny, and the Tooth Fairy were all dining at Locke-Ober's. And who do you think picked up the check?" Silence. "The answer is, the nefarious Sonny O'Reilly, because all the others are figments of your imagination!"

The fact that Senator O'Reilly laughed at this joke, Lanny Green told me afterward, did more to increase my political stature than anything else that happened in the month of March. That, and the fact that I had the chutzpah to tell it.

I sensed my time was running low, even though most eyes now were on me and the chewing had stopped. "I'm awfully sorry not to see District Attorney Gross here," I said sorrowfully. "I'm sure the reason is because he has been getting out and palling around recently with a whole new group of people he hasn't seen in eleven years." I paused. "They're called *voters*." I handed the mike back to O'Reilly before being asked.

The consensus, while not unanimous, was that Gross would have done better to have been there.

chapter five

Plum Island and the Back Bay

I was having to learn how to run and chew gum at the same time. Lucky I'm not a Republican.

On a Saturday in April, Mullally the private bird-watcher reasserted himself and Emma Gallaudette was prevailed on to guide me to Plum Island. My beloved Chevy Blazer, always sensitive to my moods, hummed over the Mystic Bridge, north on Routes 1 and 95 to Newbury.

We were not disappointed. The island carpeting was thick with swarms of goldfinches, and the warblers—black-throated blue, myrtle, and Blackburnian—were out in force.

"They're so bright!" Emma cried delightedly.

"It's the spring fashion rollout," I explained. "Their feathers are brightest just after they change color for the trip north."

"They're so lucky!" Emma said. Then, without warning, "I dare you to go in the water for one minute."

There was a pretty stiff wind along the beach and it was seasonably nippy. Notwithstanding, Emma unselfconsciously stripped down to a white two-piece bathing suit that looked like underwear, or not even. This body English was good enough for me, and I prepared to dive in.

When I dropped my billfold on my shirt, Emma picked it up, withdrew its contents, about four hundred dollars in twenties—I carry a lot of cash, no sense being caught short—and threw them into the air over her head, squealing "Wheeeeeeee!" She did it to see me scramble, and I did. She folded her arms in front of her, uh, self, and regarded me beatifically as I lunged for every last Jackson.

"'The gods to each ascribe a differing lot/some enter by the portal, some do not,'" she said mincingly.

I didn't know what the hell she was quoting, and I didn't care. I wanted to make sure I got the Jacksons back. I looked at Emma, but didn't say anything. This young lady was a life force. I haven't really regained my balance since I met her. Not that I want to.

The water was way too cold, and we didn't stay long. On the trip back Emma was bubbling. "Look at those people! I want to help them bale those sticks! Look at those kids in the quarry! I want to climb with them! I want to dive. Why aren't they diving?"

Even a pig farm in Rowley, littered with piles of tires and abandoned cars, met with favor. "I love those rusting car hulks," she enthused. "They're so organic. It's as though the car has gone from steely death to rusty life. Don't they look happy in all that mud? They remind me of those big stupid dogs who don't have to work and catch game, they just lie around the kitchen all day long and eat and sleep."

"Really stupid dogs."

"Very stupid. And I love these electricity towers and high wires and transformers up there. They look as though they have an inner life. When they escape their metallic phase, maybe they'll be giant insects."

Wow, I said to the Blazer's dashboard—one of my closest confidants. Then I thought I saw an opening. "Seat belt stuck?" I began to lean over to "help," i.e., get a better whiff of the Chanel No. 5 that had gone on between the beach and the car, along with Emma's lucky roughwear. But she was too quick. With one motion, she zoomed the metal clip back to ground zero on the door side and rezoomed it into the buckle, which still enragingly divided us. "It just wants a running start," she explained sympathetically. She was taking the part of the wretched seat belt clip.

I dropped her off chastely at 5:00 P.M. at her apartment building on Maple Ave. in Cambridge, having elicited the promise of a workday luncheon. On Sunday, I did two morning talk shows, one TV and one radio, then canceled a drop-by at a seniors' picnic in Revere and a neighborhood crime watch meeting in Winthrop, and spent a miserable afternoon trying unsuccessfully to concentrate on TV sports. When I can't concentrate on TV sports, I know I'm near death from some cause.

Most of Monday morning I sat doodling at my desk, figuring if this creature was sympathetic to burned-out cars and telephone transformers and seat belt clips, maybe she could be persuaded to be sympathetic to me. I resolved to put on my best metallic air when we got together for lunch.

We were scheduled for half past noon at L'Ananas on Newbury Street in the Back Bay. Emma was waiting in the vestibule. I got the warming smile. I noticed one of her temples had surrendered to the air a crenellation of blond hair. She shook my hand.

We had to wait half an hour for a table. I was never so glad I had failed to make a reservation. We sat at the mahogany bar, whose beauty I had overlooked on many previous occasions. I ordered a bottle of Pouilly-Fumé. Emma gave a little shimmy on her barstool. She apparently favored Pouilly-Fumé.

Suddenly she was all business. "Explain to me again about those police corruption cases in New York. You were telling Ruthie Truslow the other evening."

Okay, I said to myself, the lady is serious. I remembered her murderously quick summary of movements on the Hong Kong stock exchange, puncturing an otherwise doughy conversation. So, police corruption it's going to be.

To Emma I said, "It was virtually endemic in many precincts. Listening to the wiretaps, you realized there was a whole different world going on around you, one of which ninety-nine point nine percent of the population is thankfully ignorant. It was like putting on a special pair of glasses and seeing that the people on the street were actually animals. The gay bar owner was a startled fawn, maybe, and the guy in the blue uniform with the big smile was actually a scaly dinosaur."

"Were all the dinosaurs the same?"

"Oh, no. There were grass eaters and there were meat eaters. The grass eaters just went along with the system and munched on a few illegal weeds every now and then. But the meat eaters, once they got their hooks into a guy, they wanted to bleed him dry, if not tear him limb from limb. Even while they were handling him, they wanted him to introduce them to other guys and dolls, so they could tear into those others, too. They just couldn't get enough."

"Right, I understand. I like to wear those glasses, too. Dinosaurs is the correct angle. And I don't think it's just cops. There's a huge big fat old partner in the probate department at my office who I've always thought of as a diplodocus, which I think was a vegetarian. They lived in Colorado, near where my cousins are now. I've always liked them because they were absolutely enormous and they didn't eat anything more than an inch long. And then, of course, the managing partner is an allosaurus, all teeth. He's the biggest business producer in the office, but he's not really happy unless he's also stealing cases from other lawyers so he can get the origination fee on them, too."

She took a small swallow from her second glass of wine.

"I don't think it's just individual people, either," she continued. "Sometimes I sense something animate lurking in the current of a conversation, or the mood of a crowd. You get the feeling something's going to happen, something's going to pounce, even if you don't know which person is going to be its instrument."

Emma was racing ahead of me, so I chuckled and said I wasn't sure all of this made too much sense. Of course, that was a lie. I was on contact high. It was a downer when Tony came to tell us our table was ready.

After seeing Emma seated with her back to the wall, I settled into deep leather to enjoy more of the same fare, but her thought or mood had flown by. Maybe it was a pterodactyl.

"Perhaps allegories are more interesting than useful," she said modestly. "But I have a far more useful theory, which explains conclusively why people sometimes drink to excess. It even accounts for the origin of the 'Roman toast.' Would you like to hear it?"

I allowed as how I would, in fact, like to hear it.

"My thought is, we have all these channels of energy surfing through us—libidinous impulses, I think Freud would call them—and they are all interchangeable. One is to succeed at work, another is sex drive—if it exists, of course—another is the urge to run for public office, another is whatever makes you have ten drinks and blow it out your ear, another is wanting to jump and play, another is writing a book, another is shooting an elephant, another is making a hundred million dollars, another is self-destruction, you get the drift. If sex was compulsory three times a day, the murder rate would be zero, and so forth.

"And, candidly, if my good husband Elijah Low had not been in Thailand and Hong Kong for the past three months, I don't think you would've seen me downing those nasty stingers at the Truslows'. Not that that's of general interest, of course." She had a gulp of Pouilly-Fumé.

"No, no, of course not, no interest at all," I mumbled. Then I added, nodding, "Three months is a long time to be away."

"Oh, listen, business comes first with Elijah. His favorite saying, in fact, is 'Business is business,' which means it's okay to screw a cat, if you're doing a deal. He's told me more than once that he would absolutely kill someone and saw them in half, if it was necessary for business reasons."

"Sounds like a lot of people I used to know, in New York! How did you, um, how did you all get together? You don't really strike me as the saw-your-buddy-in-half type."

Another gulp. I motioned for a second bottle. Tony had it already chilled and open. Emma glared at her glass as he refilled it. She knew the wine was friend and enemy.

"My stepmother and Elijah's entire family were very much opposed to our getting married, which was a big plus. She was against it because he's twelve years older than I am—he just turned forty—and because he's Chinese, which wouldn't bother her except it means he's not in the *Social Register*. Literally! I kid you not. Then they, his family, were against it because they didn't understand how he could take up with a dissolute round-eye—they think all round-eyes are dissolute—and, of course, they wanted him to live in Taipei or Hong Kong."

"Those are just a terrific set of reasons to get hitched," I said, laughing. She laughed, too, then turned matter-of-fact.

"Also I thought I was pregnant. Turns out I wasn't. Later, when I did get pregnant, Elijah had just quit teaching and thought we weren't ready. So I, uh, went along. . . ."

"Oh. Sorry."

"No, I'm sorry. You didn't need to know all that. Anyway, despite that last thing that I passed over without mentioning, Elijah and I are both Catholic, so I don't think we're going anywhere soon—like Splitsville, I mean. And he is a good provider."

"You don't need a provider."

"I know." She was looking at the table.

"How does he make the money?"

"I'm not entirely privy to what gives him the value added in these deals. I knew a lot more about him before he went into business. My best guess? Some kind of semiorganized crime. Not straight up, like La Cosa Nostra, but some kind of understanding with the governments involved, with money changing hands."

This was fairly chilling. "Not the worst guess I ever heard," I said. "But with all deference to the central role of a stepmother's opposition, how do you sit still for that?"

She blinked, quick on the down, slow on the up. "Oh, listen, it's all just conjecture. And besides, buster, I happen to be one tough broad, in case you hadn't noticed. In fact, Ruthie Truslow and I founded a 'Raptors Club. We're the only members. We're velociraptors. We're rapacious; rapacious toward men, and specifically greasers. We don't see why society girls shouldn't go slumming; it's perfectly accepted around here that society men do it."

"You really think men will do anything you say, just because of sex?"

"Yep. Well, within reason."

I nodded, absorbing this.

"Ruthie told her father about the 'Raptors Club and he was absolutely wild. 'She's barely discovered the meaning of the word,' he said to a man at the Somerset, 'and now she wants to *give* it away!' Ruthie has him turned every which way but loose. She's twice as smart as he is, although he wouldn't even let her go to a four-year college. She lived in Africa for two years, studying monkeys. She has a lot more to say about anthropology than you would think from the other evening. I love that stuff. When the *Times* has something on page one about a find at Olduvai Gorge, they can throw away the rest of the paper, as far as I'm concerned."

"How often does your club, uh, go into action?"

"Oh, my goodness, we don't actually *do* any of this, we just talk about it, so the guys won't have all the fun. We've even invented two unshaven handymen, Russ and Roy, who do odd jobs around the neighborhood on Beacon Hill, and we tell people at work—at least I do, Ruthie doesn't work, her father would never permit it, but she tells her friends—that we have to leave the office, or leave the brunch or whatever, because we're going to have a 'nooner' with Russ or Roy at a Single Room Occupancy down below the

State House on Beacon Hill. Some of those places do rent by the hour, you know, so people believe us."

"Russ and Roy, huh?"

"Yes."

"Which one's your favorite?"

"Roy. He's a real greaser," she added wistfully.

I thought of the Cook's tour conducted by Ruthie during the cocktail "hour," her lewd army of missionaries, frontiersmen, and aborigines. I had a hunch I had been the victim of an elaborate put-on. Or was it?

There was a rather awkward silence and I idiotically repeated myself: "Well, I still think three months is a long time to be away." From you, I obviously meant.

"You're kind to say so. They say that sex is fifty percent of a good marriage and a hundred percent of a bad one, so I frequently tell myself I must have the best marriage on the East Coast."

"I've heard about those percentages, too. I've often thought I might settle for a so-so marriage, just to get to seventy-five percent." This got a chuckle, so I thought we might be out of the danger zone. We leaned back in our chairs. I let my shoulder muscles relax.

"Let me show you the Quabbin," I said.

"I'd love to," said Emma. "I'd love to see where your father grew up."

Nobody had ever said that to me before. But then, I had never let anybody come close to having a chance to say it.

chapter six

How to Make a Thirty-Second Spot

Martin Gross and the establishment had pretty much tried to ignore me, once the word seeped out that the unions were going to run me against him in the primary. Always the best opening strategy for an incumbent: pretend you can't remember your opponent's name.

The good news was that my gibe at the absent district attorney at O'Reilly's breakfast was lovingly reported by both Boston dailies, and two of the networks even had a clip of me doing the Easter Bunny/Tooth Fairy joke on the evening news. We heard that the "Gross people," as we called them, were livid about this, even trying to sell reporters on the notion I had taken a low blow at him because he wasn't there to defend himself. The media folks weren't buying at all: name of the game, DA, 80 percent of life is showing up, kid showed up, you didn't. Besides, the reporters wanted a race. Much is forgiven anyone who relieves the desperate boredom of the working press.

District Attorney Gross was not without allies in the media, however, and they came at me hard on the experience issue throughout the spring: I was thirty-two years old, no prior public office, he was a quarter century my senior, twenty-one years of spotless service to the people of the Commonwealth.

The one thing I had going in my favor is that unlike most first-time candidates, I was comfortable on my feet in front of an audience. Not too many political newcomers have tried thirty-five jury cases to verdict and defended them on appeal. So Lanny had me out two and three times a night, giving my stock anticorruption speech.

In late April, there was a huge cattle show at Florian Hall, candidates for all offices, local, state, and federal. Lanny came and stood by the wall at the back. Gross no-showed. I succinctly presented the case for repeal of the corruption tax. During the mix-and-mingle afterward, I could see Lanny was not satisfied. He asked me to meet him at the police union headquarters, opposite the State House, the next morning at ten.

We were both on our fourth cup of coffee when I arrived. The conference room had one table, six chairs, no windows, an unspeakably dirty floor, and about a million stale cigarette butts. A nearly full wastebasket stood in the corner, in the middle of an overflow pile of Styrofoam coffee cups. Somebody had had fun, sighting in an imaginary Styrofoam pump gun. I felt right at home. Neither of us sat down. I said I thought I had been well enough received at Florian Hall.

"Not enough to move the vote, Boss," said Lanny.

"You're good, you're real good, but all they know about you is you're against evil. Maybe you're eloquently against evil, but Martin Gross is against it, too, and they know his name better."

"So, what should I do, come out for evil, stand out in the crowd, everybody remember me?"

"We gotta peel the onion."

"What?"

"We have to take the layers off you, strip away the rhetoric, strip away the appearance, 'til we get at some facts, some stuff you actually did, that people can relate to. Snaggle-toothed facts, details that will stick in their memory whether they want them to or not. So they'll think they know you. Later, we can get them to like you."

"Great. I was born in Brooklyn in 1963—"

"That's not a snaggle-toothed fact. You ever heard of Earl Pottinger?"

"Yup. Isn't he that housepainter who got elected governor of Idaho with a white-supremacist, militia-type campaign? Abolish the federal government, et cetera?"

"Right. What else do you know about him?"

"Nothing."

"Okay. Now I'm going to tell you a story about Earl Pottinger, and in thirty seconds it's going to be impossible for you ever to think the same way about him again. Ready?"

"Set. Fire."

"This was the thirty-second spot they used in his first campaign, in 1976. It was the first thing the people of Idaho ever learned about Earl Pottinger, unless he happened to have painted their house for them. Guess what? They didn't open with a clip of old Earl painting a house, with a voiceover: 'This here is Earl Pottinger, he's a housepainter and he'd like to be your governor.'"

"They didn't?"

"No, they didn't. They opened with a shot of Earl and his missus, sitting in their own living room, watching television."

"Packs a real wallop."

"Wait. 'This is Earl and Carla Pottinger,' says the announcer. 'On December 19, 1966, Earl and Carla saw a television program about a boy named Ernie, who wanted to be adopted, who wanted a family. This is Ernie. Ernie has cerebral palsy.' And they show a clip of Ernie on television, his mouth all twisted and his arms waving around saying, 'I want a home for Christmas.' Ernie is about ten years old."

I felt something clutch at my throat.

"You all right, Boss?"

"I'm fine. Just go ahead. Please continue."

"The announcer says, 'Well, when Earl and Carla saw Ernie on television, Earl turned to Carla and said, "Carla, we're going to adopt that boy before Christmas, and raise him as our own son." And Earl and Carla got in their Chevrolet'—and they show the Chevy, and believe me it ain't no late model—'and drove *six hundred miles* to meet Ernie and bring him home in time for Christmas in Idaho.'

"Then they switch to a present-day shot of Earl.

It's a casual outdoor shot, tight on his face. 'Hi, I'm Earl Pottinger.' Nothing more, no 'I'm running for governor' or anything. Just 'I'm Earl Pottinger.'

"Then the camera backs up, and you see old Earl is standing in his yard, with one arm around Carla. He says, 'This is my wife, Carla.' There's a fence behind them, but it hasn't been painted in a long time. And I bet you can guess where his other arm is."

"I believe I can." I whispered this, so my voice wouldn't crack.

"His other arm is around a young man. He says, 'And this is our *son*, Ernie Pottinger. We adopted Ernie ten years ago and he's been with us every Christmas since. Ernie has worked hard, and this fall, he's going to *college*. Ernie, your mom and I are so proud of you.' And the final frame is a close-up of Ernie smiling a kind of twisted smile at Earl, and you can tell he's pretty proud, too. Then the screen dissolves into a simple black-and-white message: 'POTTINGER FOR GOVERNOR.'

"Now, do you feel the same way about Earl Pottinger as you did a minute ago? Terry? Hello?"

"No, Lanny, I don't."

"So. Tell me a story. Tell me a story about yourself. Tell me a story that will make people not feel the same way about you, that will make people remember you, personally."

One thing I was damned sure of. I wasn't about to tell Lanny or anyone else about the group home or the foster home. No sense starting an argument when I knew I would never give in.

"What kind of a story?"

"I won't know until you tell me. Gross says you don't have any experience. That's not quite true, you were in the U.S. attorney's office for seven years, as I understand it. Tell me stuff you did. Don't think thirty-second spot, just tell me stuff you did, stuff you liked, stuff you're even proud of. I'll worry about the thirty-second spot."

I was relieved to have Lanny's curiosity directed at my professional life, rather than personal background. So I told him. I told him how during my first three years in the U.S. attorney's office, I might as well have been a state prosecutor, it was all street crime. My second summer, there was a ton of arsons, mostly Dumpster fires, all over the city, almost every night. No injuries, medium property damage, but lots of "sirenes"—as sirens are universally called in law enforcement—and huge headlines. Agent from Alcohol, Tobacco and Firearms goes to TV news producer he is sweet with, arranges to sit down and view all the rushes of these fires, including what never aired. Mostly it was just sparkies, they follow the sirenes for any blaze. Both the cops and firefighters pretty well know who they are. Some famous people have been sparkies, perfectly legit. The conductor Arthur Fiedler, for example. But here's this one guy, shows up at five fires in different parts of the city on five consecutive nights, and in fire number four he seems pretty well along into the evening, he's sitting on a fence, and he takes out a .38 and begins whipping it around over his head. Retard, pause, zoom close up: it's a police service revolver.

Come to find out, a bunch of laid-off firefighters, with the help of this housing authority policeman, were setting all these blazes to call attention to the need for the mayor to rehire the laid-off firefighters and their brethren. They didn't have any sistern.

For once, the judge saw it our way at the end of the case. Normally, an arson with no injury and no monster property damage will get you a "baseball" sentence at most: one, two, or three years. Even with multiple offenses like this, I would have hoped only for "hockey" sentences: five, six, seven, eight. But the honorable Ferdinand Sanspeur was offended by their recklessness, and we got *basketball* sentences on these guys: thirty-six, forty, forty-eight; and twelve for the first guy to turn. Well, okay, so girls' basketball.

"Basketball sentences, I like it, I think we can use that. We'll lose the girls' basketball part. How about corruption cases? Press likes nothing better. Your stump speech is good, but bring it back to real life, give me names, bodies, dog tag numbers."

This too came easily. The growth stock when I was a fed, as I told Lanny, was Asian organized crime. Organized crime can't live without public corruption. Rudy Giuliani had all but wiped out the first two levels of La Cosa Nostra and Italian organized crime, with the Commission case and the Pizza case and the mopping up on the *capos* of the Genovese, Gambino, Colombo, and Lucchese families. We had guys who had been plug-ugly soldiers when I started out, vying with each other for *caporegime* honors. I'm not saying they were fish in a barrel, but pretty close. The Asian

O.C. cases were something new, something to keep the mind alive.

My first taste of Asian O.C. involved hoisin sauce, which is the thick plum stuff you have with moo-shi pork, one of my favorites. The U.S. Customs Service enforces Food and Drug restrictions on the amount of animal waste that can be contained in food products shipped from Hong Kong to the U.S. There was a food broker named Hiram Tsui, a self-styled "expediter," who believed these restrictions to be bad for his constitution, or at least his profit margins. Word on the street was he had paid off enough city inspectors to get unlimited amounts of Chinese rat shit into the hoisin sauce that the ladies and gentlemen of the jury might be enjoying at any moment with their moo-shi pork or scallion pancakes. But Tsui was very hinky.

I helped out the U.S. Customs investigators with a lot of luck and a little acting ability. I didn't know Chinese, but I knew Chinatown. I knew every street. I began to do a little extra hanging out around the Golden Horn after hours. I formed a platonic relationship with a showgirl by the name of Lucy. She was filled with false jocularity, like a professional fundraiser. She told me she had many acquaintances in the import-export trade who did a lot of business on the docks. I said that was quite a coincidence, because I had a friend who was a city Customs inspector who also worked on the docks. I was stirring my mai tai with a straw and looking straight into it. I could feel her eyes on me.

I threw down the straw irritably, took a wanton

gulp of the mai tai, and looked her full in the face, having suddenly remembered something. I let my own face go slack, stupid. "Actually, he's kind of a jerk," I said. "He's got a really steady job with the city, but he's always complaining he doesn't get paid enough. I think his problem is he wants to support a girlfriend or something."

Lucy was suddenly interested in her nails. "What's his name?" she asked, stifling a yawn. I told her. I didn't mention that his other name was Stephen Chu or that he was an undercover agent of the U.S. Customs Service.

Hiram Tsui wound up paying Special Agent Chu two hundred and fifty dollars, on camera, to look the other way. Got three years to serve. Good hit. The Customs guys made me an honorary special agent. I've still got the plaque.

"This is great, Boss. You know where we're going to hang that plaque?"

"Where?"

"We're going to hang that sucker right on the wall of the press briefing room when we finally get our own headquarters. Any more corruption cases?"

I was happy to share. We had an undercover operation on a bad INS inspector at the airport. On tape, in color video and audio, he palmed six hundred dollars to take a walk while a mound of forged passports and nonimmigrant visas attached itself to a bunch of newly arrived Chinese "hostesses." These were soon-to-be prostitutes, average age sixteen, all of whom had been advised that prostitution in the United States was completely optional on their part, and also entirely legal and heartily approved of by American society. They couldn't speak English and they had no options when their sponsors in the tong played bait-and-switch on them.

They made great witnesses, though, even through an interpreter. They had meant no harm. They cried a lot. They were sincere. They were very young. Their lives were ruined. The sentencing judge was a woman. The INS inspector received eighteen years to serve for his six-hundred-dollar evening. He would have been a lot better off paying the girls instead. There was a great headline in the *Daily News*: FEDS BREAK UP PROSTITUTION RING.

"Do you still have the news clip with the headline?"

"Yup."

"Do you know how many copies of it we're going to need?"

"About a million?"

"That may be a tad conservative. Any more undercover stuff?"

For sure. As I had told the cops at our first meeting, an undercover guy or a wire is the only way to get "inside," with so-called victimless crimes like narcotics or bribery.

The city cops knew more about the Chinese gangs and triads than the feds did, being closer to the bricks, the pavement. The two most knowledgeable were Paul Slifka and Rudy Solano. Slifka died early of leukemia, leaving three kids, but he had provided for them. He was a prolific producer of cases. He had a baby face,

and for some reason, that was like catnip for the dealers. The three of us—Slifka and Solano and I—must
have done a dozen buy-bust cases with the white stuff,
Southeast Asian heroin. I think it actually helped that
neither Paul nor Rudy spoke any Chinese: because they
were so utterly foreign to the world of the dealers, the
dealers couldn't pick up on any false notes, any holes in
their cover stories. I couldn't imagine why they would
take the risk of selling to a round-eye whom they'd
never met—at least, until I saw the amounts of cash
they carried. It was not at all unusual to find a quarter
of a million or even half a million dollars on or around
a dealer when the pinch was made. It was also not
unusual for the dealer to say something like "Look,
we're all good guys. We're bad good guys and you're
good good guys. Why don't you just keep the cash, and
we'll forget the whole thing?" That part I didn't share
with Lanny. It was a constant temptation for the police,
and nobody really liked to talk about it. Also, why burden Lanny with it? No upside.

What I did explain to Lanny is one reason you
need somebody cooperative on the inside to tell you
what the hell is going on, is otherwise you can't get
enough information to support a wiretap. So most of
the early effort is in trying to turn guys. This was where
Slifka and Solano excelled.

In one case, the Feebs—the FBI—had just about
won the hearts and minds of two street guys, Eddie Ho
and Johnny Cheng, who we thought were going to help
us penetrate the inner sanctum of the On Leong clubhouse. At the same time, Solano was pretty close to an

understanding with a thoroughly distasteful street thug named Olie Wing, a Vietnamese national but ethnic Chinese, who was into On Leong up to his armpits. Rudy had been talking to Olie for some time. The FBI guys thought he was talking with him too much, said Olie did "wet work," had actually clipped guys for rival dealers, and suggested Rudy was getting way too close to working both sides of the street. But my supervisor, Innis, said that was a classic Not Invented Here reaction on the part of the Bureau. Besides, I needed evidence. I didn't have time to reread the Marquis of Queensberry, to play "Who struck John?"

Eddie and Johnny gave the FBI enough general information so we got judicial permission for both a wire and an eyeball—a video camera—in the outer room of the On Leong clubhouse. One day, the guys at the Bureau monitoring the wire and the eyeball wished they'd been somewhere else. There's a card game going on in the front room, three guys we don't know plus Rudy's pal Olie Wing, who of course doesn't know we're watching, plus some huge Manchu-looking guy, big shock of black hair and high cheekbones, who's sitting just behind Olie and appears to be knitting a sweater. Who sails in the front door big as life but our two prize pigeons-in-the-making, Eddie Ho and Johnny Cheng, all decked out in their best bib and tucker. They are unmistakably there for the purpose of holding up the card game. Two of the other guys stand up and put their hands in the air. Not Olie. He just pushes back from the table a little. The Manchu sits there grinning like an idiot. He stops knitting.

Eddie and Johnny say, "We're sorry about this, Olie."

"I am sure," he says, cool as can be. When I viewed the tape, I expected him to reach for a Pimm's Cup at this point.

Eddie and Johnny have it all figured out. They're right-handed, so they're carrying under their left shoulders. Crossover draw, much quicker. So now they reach. But it turns out, it isn't a good plan. It's poor planning. Because the six-foot-five-inch Manchu, the maternal figure with piles of raw woolens in his/her lap, also has always had his left trigger finger on a Casull's .454 magnum, nestling under the threads. And the Manchu doesn't wait for Eddie and Johnny to explain, "Let's have the cash," though they start to.

He misses clean to the right on the first shot, grazes Johnny on the arm on the second. The Casull's in the small room is stunningly loud. There's much more space out in Freedom, Wyoming, where Dick Casull invented this gun. Anyway, Eddie freezes. Bad move. Career-altering move.

Johnny is moving, left, fast—but he's moving so fast his Sig Sauer apparently catches on a strap in his shoulder holster. No one gets a chance to ask him, because the third shot from the Casull's catches Johnny flat in the middle of his chest, rocketing him back to the wall and sending a geyser of blood in the Manchu's direction. Or maybe the blood just stays where it is and the rest of Johnny is flung back from it, I couldn't really tell from the video.

Eddie witnesses this event from the floor, up close

and personal, and decides he can subtract three from five and he doesn't much care about the Sig Sauer that is probably stuck in his axillary hairs at this very moment. Back to the wall, hands straight in the air, he pushes himself up gradually, by his legs, never taking his eyes off Olie's, never looking at the Manchu, smiling a deepening smile, as it goes on almost a conspiratorial smile. "None of this is personal, Olie."

The fourth offering from the Casull's hits the plywood wallboard four inches to the right of Eddie's head, and he begins laughing hilariously, in hopes it's a warning shot. But when you're shooting a gun from your crotch, it usually takes a round to sight in. All these shots have taken two, two and a half seconds, and the Manchu doesn't yet have the big revolver anywhere near up to eye level. It's out from under the woolens now, though. Bigger than life.

The fifth round hits Eddie in the nose. And these are soft-nosed bullets, dumdums. No full-metal jacket required in this crowd, everything very informal.

"You know what I'm liking about this, Boss?" said Lanny.

"What?"

"I like the way you instinctively put the action in the present tense. There's only one tense for thirty-second spots: present. There's only one medium of communication: telegraph. Short telegraph. Only enough pennies to pay for twelve words, sorry. And there's only one possible narrator: Walter Winchell. Anybody we hire has to just imitate Walter Winchell. Walter Winchell never used the pluperfect in his life."

"Lanny, you're not old enough to have even *heard* of Walter Winchell."

"I've got records and records of him doing radio. I listen to it instead of Sinatra, use it as a wake-up."

"You're a deeply sick person. You want I should finish?"

"Course."

It is the messiest crime scene I've ever seen, feds don't get too much violent stuff. One of the Feebs actually trips and falls in the doorway when he catches sight of Eddie's face, or rather part of it.

With a twenty-five-minute head start, Olie is well on his way to Toronto when Slifka and Solano and I arrive. The Manchu we find dead in an alley two blocks away—one .22-caliber pistol shot to the neck. We confiscate the Casull's. Manchu must have used it a lot: it has four trapezoidal holes cut in the barrel with a laser, to prevent kickback and overheating. Magna-porting, they call it.

"You don't suppose our man Olie could have had anything to do with the sudden demise of yon Manchu, do you?" I ask Paul and Rudy in the alley, deadpan.

"With some good investigative work, we might be able to satisfy the Mom test," Slifka offers, also deadpan. This stands for means, opportunity, motive. Slifka is being sarcastic. It couldn't be more obvious what happened to the Manchu if they had left a video of his execution.

Anyhow. Solano spends two days in Toronto that month talking with an associate of Olie Wing, but reports back that given the nature of the offenses, they can't even come close to a meeting of the minds.

The whole episode sours relations between the FBI and the NYPD for a good while. That's what happens when you have too many snitches: everybody falls in love with the snitch they turn first, and when they go up against each other, it puts a strain on the good guys, the law enforcement guys. The FBI agents can't believe Rudy would even try to communicate with Olie Wing after the shooting, but Rudy tells them to shove it, says nobody invited Eddie and Johnny to hold up the card game. I conclude Rudy has the better of the argument, and say so. It's a minority view in the office.

"Fascinating stuff," said Lanny, "but I can't use it in that form. Blood doesn't sell in thirty-second political spots. Or dumdum bullets. We can sure as hell use the hoisin sauce, though. I think I might open that one with an Ozzie and Harriet family eating at an actual restaurant in Chinatown, Boston landmark in the background, just to bring it home. Folks will not soon forget the idea of rat shit in their moo-shi pork. *That's* what I call a snaggle-toothed fact. That's peeling the onion, plucking the leaves off the artichoke. That's getting at the there there."

"Lanny, can I ask you a question?"

"Yeh, sure."

"How old were you when you managed your first political campaign?"

"Twelve. Speaking of which, we'd better go, we're meeting Kettaneh at the *Gazette* at noon for lunch."

chapter seven

The Quabbin

On the second weekend in May, I engineered an exquisite merger of my private worlds, past and present.

I had taken a leave of absence from Warfield & Coles to devote full time to the campaign, but I made Lanny block off that Friday night and Saturday so Emma and I could camp out at the Quabbin Reservoir and go fly fishing at dawn.

They didn't let the public in for two more weeks—the ice-out date varied wildly from year to year—but I suggested to Emma that rather than wait, it would be more fun to sneak in and borrow one of the locked public-use canoes. She agreed vehemently. Also camping out was strictly forbidden, which added more salt.

No salt was necessary, of course. I had been intoxicated with the history and waters of the Quabbin since I could remember. I knew everything about all five towns that were flooded to make the reservoir in 1938, especially my dad's hometown of Dana. They used to make palm-leaf hats there. In fact, Dana claimed to be the capital of the worldwide palm-leaf hat industry. I never had a palm-leaf hat, but I had fished over those factories many times, on summer visits to Cousin Lonna. The first time I was nine years old, only a year older than my father when he had to leave. So I judged we were separated by only a hundred feet and one year of water and time.

Prescott, Enfield, Greenwich, Dana, and Ripton. They sounded like the ultimate Yankee law firm. And they were gone, all gone! That was the greatest thing about them. It tickled my Irish heart. Of course, they knew they were going to be flooded, it's as though Pompeii knew Vesuvius was going to go, that's what fascinated me. Each town actually held *disincorporation* parties, sponsored by their respective *fire* departments—I kid you not—in the month before the waters rolled in. Like, they didn't want to be inundated *in their corporate form*. That killed me. Yankees kill me. It's not "Where's the beef?" It's "Where's the blood?"

The motto of Ripton, established in 1767, had been "Ripton—where every day is important." Ripton didn't want to go under, as it were, and it appears that two of their officials, Clayton Hawley of the board of selectmen and Seth Quisenberry, Sr., of the conservation commission, were boyhood friends of Governor Joseph Trainor. They mounted a letter-writing campaign to save their bacon and their everything else, but the Quabbin wouldn't work without Darey Pond, 95 percent within Ripton's borders, so Ripton was consigned to a mushy ash bin of history.

I still wonder about the lake trout and landlocked salmon and smallmouth bass wending their way through the beautiful brick churches in those five towns. Do they turn at all when they swim past the altar, or even nod? They surely must enjoy the church gardens of lilies, and the skies of trefoil . . .

So. Friday at a quarter past six, Emma and I and the dashboard of my Blazer were all driving west on Route 2, windows open and heater on full blast. Only way to travel. There was a high-riding pink mackerel sky, tastefully backlit from below. I decided to recount to Emma the ultimate Ripton story.

"Before they flooded the valley, they moved all the graveyards. Good Massachusetts logic: We don't mind tearing apart the world of the living, but we'll be damned if we're going to disturb the dead by covering them with water. Living be damned, the dead have to breathe! In Greenwich, they're digging up the cemetery and they hit a brass bedpost. Then another. Then two more.

"They retreat in some confusion and research the archives. Sure enough, 1821, old Ephraim Blueprint dies of the plague, in Greenwich, Massachusetts, and ain't nobody going to touch the body. So they bury him right in his four-poster, nightshirt and nightcap and all."

"What did they do in 1938?"

"Wasn't nobody wanted to disturb *that* little historical judgment, either. They did the same thing."

"That's a scream." She patted the dashboard. Then, without missing a beat, "You know what the Mile High Club is?"

I knew damn well. "No, what?"

"It's people who have, uh, enjoyed physical relations, physical congress in an airplane. I guess maybe it's limited to commercial flights. You a member?"

"Yes, of course. How about yourself?"

"You're a good actor, Terry Mullally, but not a good liar. Anyhow, I'm a double member."

"Oh, do tell." We almost hit the divider but she pretended not to notice.

"The first time was on a Qantas overnight flight back from Australia. It was actually the first time Elijah and I made love. We barely knew each other, except as teacher and student. Things were great before he went into 'business.' We were reckless because right after takeoff from Melbourne they came around and said, 'Would you like scotch, gin, or vodka?' and Elijah said gin and I said I'd have scotch, please make it two. And the stew said I wouldn't be wanting two of *theirs*, and came back and plunked down a *bottle* of Johnnie Walker Red on my tray and a bottle of Gilbey's—I hate that stuff, it tastes like soap—on Elijah's and said, 'It's an all-night flight. We'll see you in about ten hours.' It was very quiet in the back and there were lots of blankets and pillows. Afterward was the best sleep I've ever had. I love Qantas. In fact I love everything about Australia. Like those perceptive and tactful stews, for example."

"What was the other time?" I had my hands at eleven and one, holding on tight.

"In college. I'm not sure it qualifies because it might not have been over five thousand feet. I was on a forty-five-minute commuter flight from Philadelphia to Islip, sitting up front with my boyfriend, and suddenly we just sort of mentioned to each other, don't you find these close quarters just impossibly erotic? So we both had to go to the loo at the same time, and wouldn't you know? There was only one lavatory up front. That was great, too."

"Didn't you get caught?"

"Well, I think they were a little suspicious."

"Why are you telling me this?"

"These are kind of close quarters in here, too." She smiled, but quickly resumed her study of the delightful and absorbing map she had obtained from the Massachusetts Office of Travel and Tourism. My knuckles were white on the wheel.

We turned south on Route 202 for a few miles, disassembled a rotting wooden barrier at Gate 31 to the Quabbin, and bumped the Blazer through the woods all the way to the boat slip. We were into the gloaming, but I doused the lights as soon as we left the paved road. I wasn't interested in company.

You could just make out the masses of sweet william and forget-me-nots fringing the road. We passed three or four moss-lined streams, guarded by acres of skunk cabbage in the hollow. Emma loved every stone wall, loved the beautiful little stone arched bridge, loved the ee-o-lay of the wood thrush, loved a Carolina wren. She was bouncing up and down in her seat, slapping the vinyl with her hands. I hit a small tree just before the parking lot and cracked the right headlight. It didn't bother me at all. Normally it would have. We got out and walked to the water.

"This is the first time I've held hands with anyone in quite a while," I said.

"Oh, Terry. I'm so sorry," she breathed into the side of my head, and gave me a kiss on my left ear. Then she skipped ahead. "This is major cool. Way cool."

There was an onshore wind. The water was black and uncertain, like a block of slate being rearranged by a computer-assisted designer.

The eeriest part was not the video but the audio. The wind brought us a million tiny high-pitched ululations, like cicadas or tree frogs. But I was damn sure there were no cicadas or tree frogs on the Quabbin Reservoir three days after ice-out.

Emma got to the water first and unlocked the mystery. Thursday had been cold, and a thin sheet of ice had re-formed on the bay, while Friday had been warm, and it had broken into smithereens. The onshore wind drove all those slivers of ice onto the gravel, creating a deafening tintinnabulation. "Look!" she cried, making two pistols with her thumbs and forefingers. "It's like, shoot-out at the chandelier factory!"

I ran my hands up under the back of Emma's baggy blue sweater, and pressed her hard against my chest.

We borrowed a thirteen-foot Grumman canoe from the boat shed maintained by the Metropolitan District Commission during the season. It required nothing beyond wire cutters, though believe me, I was prepared for more: this was a night off I had been planning for. I had brought two of my favorite ash paddles, one double sleeping bag good to thirty below, and steak, potatoes, bread, butter, and coffee.

Emma handled her paddle more expertly than I had expected. We pulled south for twenty minutes. Barn swallows and bats flitted past our faces. They didn't seem to bother Emma. I steered us to my favorite cove, with a sandy beach and two beautiful stands of trees, one white birch and the other copper beech. Even in pitch dark, it would make me feel good to be near those trees. I knew they were there.

We dragged the canoe up into the long grass on the side of the beach, where a phalanx of big pines stood sentry duty. As soon as we got under them, there was a "WHOOSH/FLAP FLAP FLAP" from way overhead. I ducked, which was somewhat ridiculous.

"What was that?"

"Great blue heron." This was my third lie in twenty minutes. I had forgotten that a pair of bald eagles often nested near this beach. While generally I am a stickler for the truth, I make exception in matters of love and war. I did not want to admit to Emma that I had scared a bald eagle off its roost. Or, worse, two bald eagles. Talk about bad luck, that's badder than killing a spider.

In the failing light, we settled down to the serious business of dinner. I dug a three-foot pit for the fire, even though this place was visible from precisely nowhere. I think food tastes better if it's cooked in a pit. It's like a bottle of beer always tastes better if you've got it in a paper bag. I don't know why.

I put some stones in the bottom of the hollow to hold the heat, then nestled the baking potatoes in with them, wrapped in foil, and covered that layer with weeds I had scooped from the shallows. A few more stones, then fallen birch for the fire.

The fire held us like moths. "On the King Ranch they call this 'South Texas TV,'" I boasted.

"I can see why," whispered Emma, who never watched TV.

We shared a half-pint of Dewar's scotch. That is Emma's favorite, though I am more inclined to agree with Casey and Garcia that scotch going down tastes like bourbon coming up.

I heard the croak of an American bittern. I leaned back on my elbows, my legs crossed at the shins.

"Only two times I'll take a drink," I said at length. "When I'm fishin', and when I'm not."

"This is my favorite time of day," Emma said with some melancholy. "You can still see color in the sky, but the blue is so deep it's basically black. And the stuff down here—that branch, those little leaves—bleed all their own color in about ten minutes. Look, they were green and white two minutes ago, now they're silhouettes."

I rolled the scotch around in my mouth and nodded.

"People are the same way," she went on. "Look at them up close in the daytime, they're all pink flesh, every one individual. Get back aways, you can see the outlines of their personality, but they're not much more than silhouettes. Step farther back, take a really long view, you can't see them as individual people at all. They're just part of the mass. Now I can't even see that branch," she said in confirmation of her own point. There was a shriek—of agreement?—from a pileated woodpecker in the near distance.

"Oh, sure," I said. "People, leaves; leaves, people. Same thing!"

"No, silly," said Emma, and patted my hand. "It's light, distance; distance, light: same thing."

Fortunately, I didn't have to wrap my mind around that one, or try to, because the fire had burned down to where I could lay the steak directly on the coals. Perfect timing. Meat three minutes to a side, potatoes just done, one hour in the crucible. Lose the vegetables, as I do, in the woods. You can always chew on a fiddlehead or a swamp marigold, if you feel guilty or politically incorrect and want to balance your meal. I never do.

We ate everything and turned in around nine o'clock, relaxing in my outsized sleeping bag. I held Emma for a long time. It was the most natural thing in the world for us to become intimate, as we did.

"You're my thrush," I whispered, when I was sure she was asleep.

Not many stars, but I could see that south wind driving masses of clouds across the face of the moon. People, leaves, distance, light . . . I fell asleep to the beautiful liquid warbling of loons.

I rose at four, fed the fire, and put water on to boil. The breeze brought me a smell of something rank. Stronger than bear and not as strong as skunk, so probably a fox. The only scent I didn't want to pick up was cucumber: timber rattler.

I said to Emma, in a normal voice, "Time to get up." Take it from me, in the woods never touch someone who's asleep, it can cost you your life. The only surer path to death is to bring along a nice ironed white handkerchief when you're camping and shake it a couple times before you blow your nose. Whitetail flag, will be spotted by any self-respecting deer hunter at half a mile.

"But it's still dark," she whined groggily.

"That's the best time."

"To catch fish?"

"No, to be up."

"What's for breakfast?"

"You're going to catch it. Come on, get out of there."

"But it's *freezing!*" She shivered dramatically. I laughed in her face.

"Not when you start moving. Here, take some coffee. Get your hands warm, then put the mug against your neck."

In a few minutes we had the canoe on course toward two wooded islands where I knew the shelf dropped off sharply. There was a good current in the gut between them. An insect-laden overhanging limb, plus deep water, brings the big ones.

I could almost make out the hills ahead of us, the rolling shoulders of the whole reserve. This meant we were leaving the 1996 town of New Salem and entering the 1938 town of Dana. I felt layers of time glide by beneath us.

I handed Emma my eight-foot Leonard, Hardy Bros. reel, number four line with plenty of backing, 3X tapered leader, and a red and brown streamer I had tied myself: mottled wild turkey feathers for the wing, wood duck flank feathers for the shoulder, a red head and a number six hook.

"Steady as she goes," I whispered. Emma feathered her paddle like a pro, drew it in without a drop of water falling to disturb the surface. She slid my creation off the cork, checked the barb against her thumb, bent the Leonard almost double getting the leader free of the rod, and proceeded to execute the most beautiful series of false casts I have ever seen, culminating in the gossamer deposit of Old Reliable three feet from the bank, six inches from an overhanging log, and sixty feet from the canoe. I was, for want of a better word, agog.

"Did you have freshwater at your place in Wellesley?" I whispered. "Or is this the work of all those goddamn boyfriends?"

"My father," she said flatly. I had said the Wrong Thing again.

I was soon forgiven, for on the third or fourth tree we tried, there was a terrifying explosion just as Emma's perfectly delivered streamer hit the water. The Hardy Brothers all screamed in unison. I was glad I had put on extra backing the night before, glad I had double-checked the line, the leader, and all the knots. Hell, I was glad to be alive!

It was a salmon. Emma was a little rough with it at first, but she had to be, because the fish made a beeline for the submerged portion of the tree. I backpaddled furiously, and pretty soon we had the fish in open water, where it decided to treat us to an iridescent aerial display just as the first bits of red filtered through the mist.

Every time the salmon broke water to jump, Emma bowed her rod tip to the surface. The fish never got a direct pull at the reel, never got slack line, never got horsed. The fish, in short, never had a chance.

Emma netted it tail first, the way you are supposed to, and boated it with one strong motion of her left arm. It was a hen, four pounds. Emma killed it instantly with one blow to the top of the head from a length of metal pipe she had picked up off the ground in the parking lot. So I'm not the only one who can plan ahead, I thought. And wasn't it like Emma to have a metallic priest!

She cleaned the fish with a Swiss Army knife right in the canoe, as I like to do. She gave an anguished cry at the sight of the roe—all those babies!—but she tore the gills out by hand, ran her thumb under the backbone to get the last bits of blood out, and tossed the guts overboard, as any real sportsman will not hesitate to do: feeds the lake.

We were fishing to eat, so we left it at that. As I dug my paddle deep into the black water to turn the canoe, I noticed some crab apples bobbing in our wake. They were filled with those tiny worm holes. Life everywhere.

"Not far from the tree," I muttered.

"What?"

"The apple doesn't fall far from the tree."

"There are no trees here, it must be a hundred feet deep."

I let it ride. I exhaled and let everything ride. Emma paddled back to the cove.

In the light, she oohed and aahed over the birches and beeches, without any prompting from me.

We created an oven out of stones and logs, wrapped the fish tightly in tinfoil, and semibaked, semismoked it. We used the balance of our stick of butter, and Emma to my delight produced a lemon from her small pack. All around, it was a pretty good breakfast.

A barred owl hooted from far in the woods. "What's he saying?" Emma asked.

"Who cooks for you, who cooks for you?"

"Ohh . . ." She fell against my shoulder. It became necessary to put the sleeping bag back to use in the cool morning air.

I went for one last paddle by myself while Emma explored the woods in the cove. I steered a straight course over to Dana again. I like to travel over the land where my father walked as a boy, paddle a mile in his shoes. A nesting pair of wood ducks whistled by overhead.

There were lots of weeds at the surface and just below. This was too deep for water lilies, but there were various types of pondweed, plus some water plantain and grassy arrowhead. They all mean life itself for many kinds of ducks, fish, and snails. I broke off a few stems and admired the architecture of the tubers and the spiked flowers.

These weeds were reaching all the way from the 1938 floor of Dana to the 1996 surface—Dana's sky. These were the closest thing to trees that my eight-year-old father could shinny up if he took a fancy.

My face flushed. My father was reaching up to me, reaching up for me. I felt a tug. I wanted to be down there, back there. I would find myself there, with my father. My mind ran on. Distance, light; depth, time . . .

The desperate cry of a red-tailed hawk broke the silence. I paddled hard to get back to Emma. My private worlds were merging and I wanted to be on the scene.

As our canoe knifed to the north, the soft early sun was caressing the breast of the hills. Emma found them animate: "Look at that hippo! There's a rhino!" A flock of geese got up noisily from the reservoir for a day in the fields.

Looking north, Emma pointed dead ahead of us and said, "*What* is *that?*"

"That's Mount Monadnock, in New Hampshire. It's thirty miles away, but it looks like you can touch it, doesn't it?"

"It looks like you can *eat* it! It's even à la mode!"

I chuckled at this. A late snowstorm had left a residue of vanilla on the peak. Maybe I could persuade Locke-Ober's to serve Monadnock à la mode as well as baked Alaska.

"Rudy Solano has a deer-hunting spread just

south of there, near Jaffrey, three hundred acres and a heated cabin. It's off Route 202, same road as we took here, different state."

"Wow. How did Rudy get three hundred acres that close to Monadnock?"

"No idea. Family, maybe. He's had it for quite a while. I was up there with him last November, and he got a nice ten-point buck."

"What's that, a little deer with all his toes?"

"And one who wasn't on them, unfortunately."

"Oh." A frown, seen from the side. "But at least it was a him." She brightened at this thought.

"At least it was a him," I repeated. Emma was still thinking about the roe in the hen salmon she had killed. My read, anyway. A breeze hit us and her hair flew free.

We watched a pair of mergansers, high up, climb a wooded hill until they disappeared. The drake was dressed in spectacular black and white, the hen in her normal drab dun colors.

"How come the guys get all the good feathers?" Emma asked. I was impressed, but not surprised, that she knew which was which.

"It's nature's way."

"No, it's not. It's a guy thing. I mean, look who gets to wear neckties."

A guy thing. I thought of Emma in her green and red Diane Von Furstenberg cocktail dress. I couldn't get the smile off my face, so I ducked my head down and paddled strenuously.

chapter eight

It All Started with a Sandwich

Lanny wrenched me back to my public world with a telephone call at 6:00 A.M. on Monday. The first words I heard when I picked up the receiver were "Three things, Boss."

I valued Lanny's habit of skipping the salutation and failing to introduce himself. Don't complain, don't explain, never apologize, the English say; my codicil to that is never say hello, good-bye, please, or thank you if you can avoid it. I never do exit interviews. Waste of time. Go on to the next thing.

"Boss, you there?"

"I'm shaving. I'm applying Occam's razor." Actually, I had hesitated because I was afraid the telephone and the shaving cream were somehow going to combine to electrocute me—I am somewhat on the low-tech side, as these things go. I kept my fears to myself.

"Number one, we have a headquarters, 99½ State Street, second floor, over the coffee shop, next to the dentist, no window signs allowed, grungy space but big war room, which is all we really care about for field HQ. Two, the bumper stickers are in, we're planning to get five thousand on next weekend, Gross's aren't on yet, it will freak them out. Three, and most important, the Animal is Hungry. They missed you over the weekend. I know we were out of pocket, but Gross was doing avails from Jamaica Plain to East Jesus, announcing federal Byrne grants, playing huggy-body with the chief in Winthrop, kissy-face with Senator Reinhardt in Chelsea and Revere, it was enough to make you puke. So, we need to feed them more Strange Tales of Gotham. That Asian organized crime stuff stirred up the pot pretty good last week, but the Animal is feeling like it was an appetizer."

"We could give them details on the police corruption cases, those were my biggest ones, after all, but that might risk cutting us loose from our base."

"Risk we gotta run. Press is antsy. My best take, right now we're in danger of sinking beneath the waves, stature-wise. I don't want to see that in print as a *fait accompli*, once it gets set in cold type it'll be like a snowball downhill. I'll give Fay and St. Onge a heads-up that it's coming, we'll tell them it's all bullshit, would never happen here, but you gotta do what you gotta do, and so on. They'll understand, they're pros."

"Okay, I'll meet you at the headquarters at seven and give you chapter and verse on the police stuff."

"Swell, you can say hello to the volunteers."

"At seven Monday morning?"

"Campaign never sleeps, Boss. Gotta have clips

and wire stories faxed to our network before anybody goes into a breakfast meeting. Theme of the day, theme of the week. Monday's the key day. I'll have double Starbucks waiting for you, one milk, half a sugar, right?"

"See you there."

"Not if I see you first. No, just kidding." Click. Lanny couldn't turn it off, but he sure knew how to press the button for the next call holding. He had six buttons on his phone, and he needed them.

In terms of choice real estate, our new head-quarters was roughly on a par with Mudville, Casey's barn. The floor was green linoleum, the windows were so grimy you couldn't see the fancy new office building across the street—actually, maybe that was so they couldn't see in—the plumbing backed up constantly, and the desks and chairs were not only unmatched, rickety, and outright missing body parts here and there, but were so few and far between that many people did their telephoning from the floor. I named my chair Peter Stuyvesant for good reason, but I never sat in it, so it didn't matter.

Lanny was right about the place being alive at 7:00 A.M. Four things we did have: telephones, forty of them; copiers; fax machines; and volunteers. Kids with wide-open, expectant faces, women who hadn't worked in five years because of young children and were now dying to get out of the house, a few "good government" types who liked my political profile, and a few whom Martin Gross had crossed in some way. Incredibly, they all seemed to get on fine and nobody complained about the slovenly working conditions. Nothing like a single unifying purpose to meld an organization.

Half the walls were covered with multihued maps of Suffolk County, ward by ward and precinct by precinct, with hundreds of color-coded pushpins indicating key operatives, beachheads, and strongholds. Not too many of the last type. All the remaining wall space was filled with posters, bumper stickers, buttons, and old newspaper headlines from campaigns current and long past—the political equivalent of subway graffiti, and about as well organized.

Lanny was sitting at a three-legged desk in one of the two smaller rooms, holding a phone to each ear. To his right, he said, "Yes, Rusty, that's what we need you to do. Signature papers for the six highest-numbered wards, then later we can talk about strategy. I *know* that's where Martin Gross lives, but it's also where *you* live, my friend. Cheers!"

To my surprise, he was able to remove the phone from his right ear—it had seemed to be affixed there. To his left-hand listener, he said, "I was just getting rid of that kid Rusty Dean. He's a plant. Says he's all disappointed with Gross's performance, won't ever work for him again, wants to come in, work at headquarters full-time, help us with strategy. Sure, pal. I checked him out. Complete bag job. Later for him! But I don't want them to know we know, 'cause I can't afford to burn my source."

Lanny listened for a moment. "Where does who work?" he barked. "Oh, the source? He works at Gross headquarters." He hung up.

"There's your Starbucks, Boss. Let's hit it." He looked at both his hands, to make sure there was not a telephone in one of them, the way people will sometimes check behind their ears for a pencil. Seeing the coast clear, he wrapped his palms around a cardboard cup and leaned toward me.

I began by explaining to Lanny that my big police corruption investigation was actually suggested by the cops and asked whether that was good or bad.

"That's good, very good. Cops are the heroes of the crooked cop story. I love it already."

I told Lanny I was having a beer with Garcia and Casey, my deer-hunting pals, talking about Operation Greylord, the undercover case on the Chicago judges, and Garcia says, "You really want to make a mark on this town, you should launch Operation Submarine."

"Naval shipyard? Spy stuff?" Lanny was hopeful.

"That's what I thought, too." Garcia says no, submarine, like submarine sandwich, heroes.

"First thing Scotty ever taught me about bad cops," Luis says. "It all starts with free sandwiches. Pretty soon, the joint is open a little late, maybe some of the patrons be wearing short shorts and halter tops and be hanging around a lot and bingo! There's a ten-sky in the wax paper. Maybe there's a slight beef about underage sales, presto! It's a Jackson, or a couple Jacksons.

"Then maybe there's a beef about a video poker game in the back, or not even, just there might be. For the gay bars, there doesn't need to be *actual* trouble.

Just, might be. Makes sense! Step up the uniformed patrol activity outside, fags of course just love it—increases the traffic considerably, everybody wants to walk the gauntlet, get pinched, maybe even get outed on TV!

"So next thing you know it's not a tensky," says Garcia, "and it's not Old Hickory, and it's not wrapped in wax paper and it's not related to mealtime. It's a regular thing, and it happens inside, behind a closed door, you'll never get rained on and you'll never get spotted and everybody does better and everybody's happy.

"The commissioner and the mayor and the DA are happy because the crime rate is falling, thanks to their personal efforts. After-hours and sales to minors, hooking, illegal gaming, even fire and safety beefs, they're all way down.

"And you know who else is happy? Your everlovin' wife and kids are happy, because you're not spending half your time explaining how you can't afford to take them to goddamn Bertucci's.

"So don't sit around on your big Irish arse," says Garcia with pleasure, "waiting for nice-guy cops like me and Casey and Paul and Rudy and Domenic and Simma to bring you lay-down one-ounce buy-bust cases. Go see Burroughs and get yourself assigned with all the beautiful Yales and Harvards to Official Corruption."

Which is what I did.

Unfortunately, it wasn't just the idea for Operation Submarine that came from the cops; it was also the evidence, or "predication" for the investigation. And it involved an old friend of mine, as I told Lanny: Sergeant Joseph Anthony Ballaster, NYPD.

Here I began to choose my words with care. I didn't want to burden Lanny with information that couldn't under any circumstances be shared with the press.

"I hadn't seen Ballaster to speak of in more than a decade when this IRS report crossed my desk." I handed Lanny my file copy.

May 10, 1994

APPLICATION FOR FULL FIELD INVESTIGATION

Anthony J. Rehovek, Special Agent, Internal Revenue Service, being duly sworn, deposes and states as follows:

1. I am an investigative law enforcement officer of the United States empowered by law to conduct investigations and to make arrests for offenses enumerated in Titles 18 and 26, United States Code. I have participated in investigations involving organized crime and official government corruption in the New York City/New Jersey area for the past twelve years.

2. There is probable cause to believe that violations of Title 18, U.S. Code, and Title 26, U.S. Code, have been committed, are being committed, and will continue to be com-

mitted in the Eastern District of New York
and the Southern District of New York by
the following individuals:

A. Patrolman Sean Scully, N.Y.P.D.

B. Sergeant Joseph A. Ballaster, N.Y.P.D.

C. Patrolman FNU LNU, N.Y.P.D.,
Caucasian male, approximately six
feet one inch, light build, red hair,
assignment/precinct unknown.

3. The aforesaid violations consist of a
systematic pattern of shakedowns and
extortion of owners and operators of
homosexual bars and sex clubs, so-called,
and concealment of the monetary pro-
ceeds of such shakedowns and extortion,
all under color of official right and in
violation of Titles 18 and 26, U.S. Code.

4. The statements contained in this affidavit are
based on information provided by three confidential informants, CI-1, CI-2, and CI-3,
previously determined to be reliable, and on
my experience and background as a Special
Agent of the Internal Revenue Service.

5. Authority is requested to open a full field
investigation, jointly with the Office of the
United States Attorney for the Eastern
District of New York.

/s/ A. J. REHOVEK, S.A., C.I.D., I.R.S., U.S. DEPT.
OF THE TREASURY

"I used to know Ballaster pretty well when I was a kid, so I felt as though I'd been slugged in the stomach."

"But you brought the case anyway. You prosecuted your friend and sent him to jail. You'd run over your own grandmother to uphold the law. I love it."

"Well, not so fast. Joe didn't exactly wind up going to jail, that's a, uh, potential delicacy in the situation."

"Okay, go ahead."

I went ahead. The weekly meeting of the "special investigations section," which is what we called the corruption unit, was the next afternoon. "Juicy one here, boys," said Pastore, the head of the unit, tossing copies of the application on the table. "Thank God it's the IRS and not the Bureau, so maybe we can get some work done without spending half our time arguing about who hung the moon."

"Yeah, love those IRS cases," said Rod Owen. "Six and a half years through the bureaucracy to the preindictment stage, we're all back in private practice, maybe they'll get three months on some guy on a plea."

"You ever hear of a joint investigation?" said Pastore. "Sure the IRS won't appreciate bringing in the Feebs, but as long as we include a couple of tax counts against each defendant and insist on a plea to a tax count for anybody who cops out, ultimately CID will be okay." CID was the Criminal Investigative Division of the IRS. Absolutely the toughest, straightest guys in the business, and all too frequently relegated to playing second fiddle.

I was new in the unit, and I asked how do you get both sides for tax evasion in a bribery case. Meaning, if somebody's getting payoffs that should be taxable, the other guy is parting with money, not receiving it. This disgusted Pastore, who said, "*Klein* conspiracy, you idiot. Section 371."

"Maybe we'll leave that out, too," Lanny observed. "Does this get better, Boss? Do you start looking better?" I suggested I just tell him the story, he could peel the onion.

So. At that point Pastore said, "We gotta call in the Bureau," meaning the FBI. "The IRS guys got into this because of skimming, but they don't know the waterfront. Assuming the sources are okay, and FNU LNU"—that means First Name Unknown, Last Name Unknown—"is guilty as charged, you know the Bureau's O.C. Section is going to have eighty-five times as much dope on the maggots who are doing the paying. And that extra bit of dope will make the difference in winning the mind and heart of the guy who decides he'd rather play witness than defendant."

We hated to say so, because the Treasury agencies were often much easier to deal with than the FBI, but we knew he was right.

I proposed bringing in the NYPD Internal Affairs Unit, but that got no votes. "Why don't you just take out an ad in the *Daily News*, FEDS INVESTIGATING POLICE CORRUPTION IN LOWER MANHATTAN GAY BARS?" was Owen's reaction. I dropped it. Three weeks later, though, everybody reversed field.

Owen got the first chair and I got the second. I got to name the investigation. I dubbed it Operation Submarine.

"Nice, Boss. Very nice."

It turned out that Confidential Informants 1, 2, and 3 were as good as their word. The thin blue line in Area E had indeed been getting a little plumper as a result of monthly payoffs from every gay bar and sex club in the district.

Owen and I were by no means blind to the sensational possibilities of the case, and partly for that reason, we were in no hurry to involve Tarzan or his first assistant, Tom Suffern. They were both incredibly press-happy.

"Who's Tarzan?"

I explained Tarzan is what everyone called the U.S. attorney, John Burroughs, because Edgar Rice Burroughs wrote that book. Also most people thought he had had a few Janes around the office, at least in his early years. His predecessor, old Joe Davies, used to advise the new assistants never to dip their pen in company ink. Tarzan was more likely to end an afternoon meeting with AUSA's by yawning and saying, "Believe I'll take me a dip in the secretarial pool." That generally cleared the room.

"Probably can't do a TV spot around that, Boss, but tell me more about your guy there, the top guy."

Burroughs, I said, was a good-looking man, or at least aristocratic looking, even if he had run to fat somewhat in his fifties. He was from a prominent Long Island family. His maternal grandfather had been a U.S. senator from Maryland. He oozed money, or rather his voice oozed money. You knew instinctively money would never be a problem for anyone within the sound of that voice. I liked hanging around with Burroughs. I didn't ask him about cases, I asked him about the stock market. I think he welcomed that as kind of a respite from his routine. He had been the United States attorney in Brooklyn for twenty-two years.

"Twenty-two years in the same job? Yecchhh! Okay, back to business."

As I told Lanny, we considered applying for a wiretap, but the whole mix was pretty combustible, and there was some evidence that the cops on the take were already hinky, so we weren't sure we had the time. Besides, that would have involved everybody from Burroughs to the pencil-necked geeks in Washington, D.C., who had to approve all wiretap applications. The assistant attorney general in charge of the Criminal Division was a notorious nitpicker; he once sent every U.S. attorney in the country a copy of the chapter from Fowler's *Modern English Usage* on the proper placement of commas. That we didn't need.

We also considered the possibility of sending a UCA—meaning an undercover agent—in on one of the guilty parties, but we couldn't exactly dress him up in the uniform of a patrolman, he'd be made in five minutes, and we couldn't send him in from the gay bar side without the cooperation of management.

It was clear, therefore, that we had to roll somebody. Owen was for putting the pincers on Virgil Tortue, owner of the Piccadilly Circus. Virgil had two priors, one for ITSP—interstate transportation of stolen property—with the feds, and one state morals charge, both felonies. Virgil would know that most federal judges have limited senses of humor when it comes to three-time losers. So we figured he might be on the nervous side, and be interested in cooperating in exchange for use immunity—they can't use your testimony against you—or even transactional immunity—they can't prosecute you for it, period—if he got lucky. No sense getting hooked that third time.

On the other hand, the case could be approached by trying to make the first crack on the police side. That would be unorthodox, because usually it's impossible to jam up an officer unless you have three or four men of the cloth willing to point the finger directly at him from the witness box. But if it was high risk, it was also high reward: once you have one prosecution witness in blue, the jury sees that there are people dressed in blue here disagreeing about very obvious fact questions that should not be controversial, like whether Officer X took three thousand dollars in cash from Virgil Tortue on the twentieth of every month for the last six years. This tends to undermine the credibility of the dressed-in-blue defendants, if they take the stand. And one thing we knew for certain: If a defendant police officer does not take the stand in a corruption case, he's hooked and cooked.

At that early stage of the investigation, Owen and I did not have to go to our superiors unless we wanted an undercover operation, or a wire, or full transactional immunity for a bad guy. So our Friday meetings, to review the week's progress and plot the surveillance for the weekend and the coming week, involved just us and the Bureau guys and the IRS. In that small company, I was able to carry the day for a high-risk, high-reward strategy, namely confronting my old pal Ballaster directly, and offering him use immunity in exchange for his full and unstinting help in the service of the public interest.

I also knew Tony Felice, Esquire, a former killer prosecutor who I thought Joe would probably run to, and I knew Felice to be a flexible and caring person.

"What does flexible and caring mean?"

I explained to Lanny it means a lawyer who will plead his guy out in a minute to avoid jail time, and have him roll over on everybody else, testify against them. A prosecutor's dream: and former prosecutors tend to think instantly of that possibility. As it turned out, Felice followed the book here and I myself did so later, in the Metaxas case in Boston.

Anyway, if you lived in New York that summer, you wouldn't need me to tell you what happened. We picked up Joe Balls right outside his house in Flatbush at 3:15 A.M. on a fine Sunday in June, on his way back from a round of the gay bars in Manhattan. Sure enough, he was loaded. With cash.

Joe didn't seem impressed that we had brought the FBI to meet him, but when the geek from the IRS said, "I'm jeop-ing this," grabbed the three envelopes of cash, and handed him a formal jeopardy assessment, I could see Joe's life passing before his eyes.

"You guys come in, be quiet, and don't look

around until I tell you you can, which I'm not," he said. "I gotta call Felice."

Counselor Felice was there in fifteen minutes. All he said was "You gotta letta?"

I did.

I handed Lanny my file copy of the letter.

> U.S. Department of Justice
> United States Attorney
> Eastern District of New York
> June 14, 1994

Anthony M. Felice, Esq.
Felice and DeCordova
32 Court Street
Brooklyn, N.Y.
Re: Joseph A. Ballaster

Dear Mr. Felice:

This letter sets forth an agreement between the United States Attorney for the Eastern District of New York ("the U.S. Attorney") and your client, Joseph A. Ballaster. The terms of the agreement are as follows:

1. You agree to cooperate completely with federal law enforcement agencies. You will answer completely all questions put to you. You will not falsely implicate any person. You will furnish to the government any documents or other records in your custody, possession or control, and will make yourself

available for interview by attorneys for the government and other law enforcement agents upon request and reasonable notice. You will testify completely before any grand jury, and at any hearing or trial should your testimony be requested.

2. In return for your full cooperation, as set forth above, the U.S. Attorney agrees not to use any statements or other information provided by you or any information directly or indirectly derived therefrom, or to proceed against you in any criminal case concerning the matters or things concerning which you provide such evidence, except a prosecution for perjury, obstruction of justice or making a false statement after the date of this agreement.

If you agree that this letter accurately describes the entire agreement beween you and the U.S. Attorney, please confirm this by signing in the appropriate place below and returning the letter to Assistant U.S. Attorney Terrence Mullally, Jr.

Very truly yours,
JOHN S. BURROUGHS
United States Attorney
By: /s/ Terrence Mullally, Jr.
Assistant United States Attorney
Special Investigations Section
Criminal Division

Acknowledged and agreed to:

_____

JOSEPH A. BALLASTER, Sgt., N.Y.P.D.

Witness: _____

ANTHONY M. FELICE, ESQ.
Counsel for Sgt. Ballaster

Felice didn't even try to give us a poker face. I admired that. His brow furrowed; he looked over at Joe Balls with motherly concern. "Leave us a minute," he said.

"Nothing easier," said I. "Gents, let's park on the steps." I led our retinue outside.

"Mullally, are you out of your mind? They can be flushing anything in the world down the toilet," said Curt Brusca, the lead FBI agent.

"Special Agent Brusca, with all due deference, if Joe Balls had anything incriminating in that house, which he shares with his wife and one of his two daughters, it would have been flushed down the toilet so long ago, it would be in Australia by now."

We were interrupted when the door opened and Tony Felice motioned us in. We didn't even have time to sit down.

"You got a deal," he said.

The rest is, as I said to Lanny, if not history at least newspaper stories, generally page one above the fold.

I handed Lanny my full file of New York newspaper clips on Operation Submarine. It was an inch and a half thick.

Eleven pleas, including six police officers, three convictions of bar owners after jury trial, one police commissioner resigned, two area superintendents transferred, one mayor sorely embarrassed, one U.S. attorney named Tarzan being touted to run for mayor of New York City. And it all started with a sandwich in wax paper!

Over the course of the next month, Lanny made sure every political reporter in Boston knew all about that sandwich. By the end of June, he felt we were making progress in closing the "stature gap" between me and Martin Gross.

What I didn't tell Lanny or the press in Boston, and what miraculously never made the papers in New York at the time, was that there were two nasty little subplots to the marvelous story of Operation Submarine.

chapter nine

Professional Courtesy

My last month in New York remains to this day a source of anxiety and bad dreams for me. The difference between having it all and losing it all really is a knife edge, in my line of work. Lines of work.

What didn't make the papers is that Burroughs and his first assistant, and about half of our office, and about two-thirds of the FBI, thought we had given away the storehouse to catch a few mice. Sure, six cops had been convicted, and four had actually gotten time, but the guy who it turned out was masterminding the pad was inadvertently given *total immunity* by an *assistant* U.S. attorney, namely, yours truly. Furthermore, without ever even suffering the embarrassment of having to testify at trial against a brother officer, he had resigned from the force and was now collecting a full pension!

Two days after the jury brought in the last guilty verdict, against poor old Virgil Tortue, Burroughs summoned me to his office. Tom Suffern was standing over in the corner with his arms folded, looking at the floor.

"Terry, you know I love you like a brother." All business. Burroughs took a breath. "We have skated big-time to this point because of the commissioner resigning, but if they ever put a good reporter on this story, who knows something about how the tenderloin district works, they are going to be wondering why the guy in charge of the pad is walking, and we are spending the people's resources conducting jury trials of poor, miserable excuses of get-a-life human beings like Virgil who probably should be beneath our notice in the first place."

"Chief, six cops go down, four go away?"

"All to the good, my son. But their superior in crime, whom you just happen to have known personally since you were in knee pants, gets everything but a letter of recommendation from us? Worse, from you? That little fig leaf won't stand up in a light wind for a New York minute."

"I made the best professional judgment I could under the circumstances and at the time, Chief. We did the office proud. I hadn't really seen Joe Balls in thirteen years. That's longer than the statute of limitations! My prior relationship with him and his lawyer had nothing to do with the decision to offer immunity."

"Appearance sucks," said Suffern.

I went on offense, maybe a mistake, but I was irritated. "You don't really mean the appearance sucks, because it doesn't," I said. "You mean, you might get criticized by the press for this—and not even rightly so. If that was our standard, we never would have brought the Whitters case, or Grimaldi, or the Seven Brokers. *Remember?*" I turned to Burroughs. "Chief, the fact is, me knowing Joe just allowed me to see the *possibility* of cracking the case on the 'official' side of the ledger, which you know and I know is nice work if you can get it."

There was a long pause. Burroughs and I stared at each other.

"I'd *like* to believe that," he said finally.

The next day, Burroughs again called me into his office. This time he was alone.

After some small talk, he introduced a new topic—nonchalantly, but I could hear the strain in his voice.

"Say, Terry," he said. "I was just rereading your prosecution memo and the supporting stuff, and there's one thing that's kind of got me puzzled about this whole set of cases. In the early weekly reports, you and Owen were kind of floundering around about who precisely all the targets might be on the police side. But after Internal Affairs of the NYPD got involved—at your recommendation—in about a week, you went right to the big seven, and you never wavered, and bingo! you were right on the money about every one of them. Those seven and no more. Everybody's story dovetailed perfectly, from that point on."

"Right you are, Chief."

"Thing is, the reports don't say anything about an internal snitch, and no approval was sought or given for a wire, and knowing what I know about the PD's Internal Affairs Unit, seems to me unlikely they outperformed the IRS and the FBI in one week. So the puzzling question is, how did you and Owen know?"

"Very sensitive source, Chief."

"Sensitive because it's illegal?"

"Intelligence wires been going on a long time, Chief. Done a lot of good over the years. Forces of Right, Forces of Evil. Good guys, bad guys."

"Intelligence wire, also known as illegal wire, also known as violation of Title III, also known as violation of oath of office, also known as felony, also known as blow every single goddamn one of your convictions sky-high if anybody in a black nightie ever got the slightest wind of it. No authorization, no court order, no minimization, no sealing application, no log, no privileges, no chain of custody, no nothing! The office would never recover." He was red in the face. "This conversation never happened. Now get the HELL out of this room."

When Tarzan made up his mind, he truly was like a bull going home. For all his force, I was not that impressed. "Chief," I said, "if the subcommittee calls me, I'll be leading them to church before we're done." Little did I know! But that's another story.

Although the blowup with Burroughs did not become public knowledge, I figured it would pretty much kill any chance I had of running for DA in Brooklyn, as I had been considering. Even if Burroughs himself kept his mouth shut, the FBI has a long memory, and can drop dimes with the best of them. So I concluded a change of scenery would do me good, and began looking around. After two weeks on the interview circuit, I landed the job with Warfield & Coles in Boston, which at least paid decently.

A number of assistant U.S. attorneys, though, knew my move was not 100 percent voluntary. I suspected I would not greatly enjoy my official farewell party.

The going-away party was an ingrained custom of the office for every departing assistant. Since there was a pretty good tradition of not bouncing people out into the snow when the office changed party hands, Democrat to Republican or vice versa, these were virtually always upbeat affairs. Sure, there were some instances where an incoming USA didn't think too highly of a particular lawyer, but that was show biz; that wasn't a fight in the family.

The division between me and Tarzan on Operation Submarine was a fight in the family. The more I thought about it, the angrier I got at him. I had practically elected him mayor of New York City! Whose side did he think I was on? And that current went both ways. I don't know whether it was because we had been close, or because he saw a lot of himself in me—willfulness, an occasional tendency to glide, usually successfully—or a combination, but Tarzan was just as ragged as I was.

Ordinarily, the first assistant or the chief of the Criminal Division would preside at these occasions. But Suffern and Hicks were both out: we were barely on speaking terms because of the situation with Ballaster's immunity. (My take was Tarzan had not even told them about the intelligence wire.) So "Dapper Peter" Darrin, a fifth-year man out of Columbia Law School who wore a gold stickpin behind flawless silk cravats, did the honors.

The party was called, as they usually were, for 5:00 to 7:00 P.M. in the basement of Stubs, an upscale sports bar within easy walking distance of the courthouse. This actually meant within stumbling distance of the garage underneath the courthouse, to which the revelers would return. Driving under is not a federal offense.

At 6:00 P.M. there were seven people in the basement: myself, Darrin, Rod Owen, one paralegal, and three secretaries including my own. I thought, "Never let 'em see you sweat," but I was frosted. I resolved if I ever found myself terminally antagonistic toward anybody in law or business, they weren't going to be able to prove it by anything I did, or at least by anything they could pin on me. I had a grateful rush at the thought that I was going to Boston, home and incubator of the "Don't get mad, get even" school of politics.

My irritation only increased when the place began to fill up around 6:40. Early enough to say they had been there, but late enough to show solidarity with the boss.

Burroughs arrived around ten minutes to seven, and Darrin took the mike at seven. The tone at these events was supposed to be all "roast," and Darrin was known for an exceptional sense of humor. But to my consternation, he played it straight. "I am particularly

pleased and honored to have been asked to preside at
these proceedings," he intoned, "because as you all
know, on anybody's analysis, on anybody's short list,
on anybody's list of one, Terry Mullally is and has been
for some period of time the decathlon champion of
this office. He may have been number two or three or
four on preparation, number two or three or four on
openings, number two or three or four on cross, number two or three or four on closings, number two or
three or four on appellate, but put them all together,
this guy comes out number one."

This was an applause line, and there was a diffi-
dent clapping from two or three of the secretaries—or
was it three or four?—which echoed cavernously in the
basement.

Darrin shrugged and called on Suffern. Suffern
started well enough, attacking me as the Master of
Misdirection in grand jury procedure, and recalling the
Asian organized crime investigation where I quite publicly walked to a three-hour lunch in Chinatown on the
day of the most critical grand jury hearing, leaving a
wet-behind-the-ears first-year assistant to take delivery
of the nightclub business records. The mob lawyers figured it must not be important if such a junior guy was
handling it, and with a sigh of relief handed over all the
original records that wound up hooking their clients.
Good story. Should have stopped there.

But Suffern was nothing if not a popinjay, so he
couldn't let well enough alone. Smirking, he relayed
truthfully but without emotion that I had been highly
recommended to the office by the NYPD. He accu-

rately quoted them as having marketed me as a "shark." He told without embellishment the story of our first two meetings, where he had basically flung in my face the overzealous recommendations and invited comment. It was true, as he said, that I had replied, "Oh, John's too kind," and "Luis is a friend."

The closer from Suffern: "So I'm sitting there thinking to myself, 'This guy's a shark? Hell, this guy's an *idiot!*'"

I'd heard it before, when Suffern and I were on the hiring committee together, and it generally got an appreciative chuckle. Because, you know, who knows? and things change and that's kind of funny.

That night it bombed. The place was so quiet nobody dared move for fear of making a noise. Suffern smiled and made as though to hand the mike back to Darrin. Dapper Peter by effusive pantomime and hand gestures indicated it was my turn now.

As I took the standing mike, four assistants left via the door six feet to my right. I made a mental note. I still remember every one of their names. I saw Burroughs look at his watch. So did everyone else.

"Thank you so much, Dapper Peter," I began. "It is likewise a pleasure and an honor for me to be here tonight, at such a happy blend of the *Night of the Living Dead* and the cantina bar scene from *Star Wars*." A couple of chuckles.

"These are occasions to just sit back and let memory roll, to reflect, to rewind and play back the tape. And I can honestly tell you: when I think of all the cases I've had over the last seven years, the agents and officers

I've had the privilege of working with, the witnesses through whom I have come to understand the complexity of sordid situations, the fellow assistants with whom I have panned for and refined this gold; when I think of the supervisors to whom we've taken our poor, meager nuggets, seeking their blessing, nay, unto the U.S. attorney himself, and beyond that, when I think of the noble gowned individuals who have been the ultimate arbiters of the worth of our productions ... When I think of all these things, I can say to myself only one thing." Here I paused. The audience was not quite sure where I was going.

"THANK GOD IT'S OVER!"

Pretty good laugh on that round.

"Seriously," I went on, "you all know that there's nothing more important to me in the world than the work we do in this office, day in and day out. And there's no more important ingredient to that work than the direction and the tone that is set from the top, as it has been set by U.S. Attorney Burroughs every day of the seven years it has been my privilege to serve the people of New York and this office. And I know that everybody in this room"—the crowd was now about 85 percent secretarial and support staff—"understands that we are a thin line, no less than the NYPD or the FBI, and we are the line that makes sure that justice gets dispensed without fear or favor." Now I saw that I had lost the audience entirely.

"And so I thank you." I was finished. Silence.

I looked over at Burroughs. Ordinarily, the boss would take the mike now for some cheery closing remarks. I had expected an appraising look, but Burroughs's eyebrows were way down. With a black gaze on his face, he gave me a half-wave from the elbow and walked out of the room.

November of 1994 was already shaping up as the most unpleasant month I had gone through since leaving the foster home, but the worst was yet to come.

I resigned from the office a week or so after the farewell party, and crated up my belongings for the move to Brighton, er, Boston. Late one afternoon, I was sitting on a barstool in the East Seventies, trying to kill an hour that just wouldn't die. Who should tap me on the shoulder but Sergeant Joseph Ballaster, NYPD, retired. In retrospect, I suppose he had been tailing me.

"Hey, Mister Big Shot!" he said. I lit up, too. We punched each other in the shoulder. "Time for me to buy you that drink we never had," he suggested. I thought he shot me a funny look, but I figured it was because he was embarrassed about his role in Operation Submarine. What the hell, I said to myself, I'm a free agent now, between jobs, no boss, I can talk to whoever I want.

I motioned for Joe to join me at the bar. "Let's get a booth," he said. That's when I knew something was coming.

We ordered Guinness.

"So!" he began falsely. "You're all set up on your own, now!"

I studied my beer. I couldn't look at him. "Yes, that's right, Sergeant. Why, what is it?"

"You're on your own now, nobody to rely on but yourself, from this point forward."

The stout had gone warm in my mouth, I couldn't swallow it. I spat it out into the glass. Now I looked at him. "Tell me," I said.

"I always told myself I would, soon as you got on your own. I've been putting off calling you, wanted you to get your legs under you. Now you've left the prosecutor's office, you don't owe anybody, you're totally on your own."

I just stared at Joe. He took a swig. It sounded like he was swallowing a frog. He put the bottle down too hard. Clunk. I waited.

"Your father didn't die in no car wreck, Terry. You got a right to know that. He was killed in a shoot-out, between some wiseguys and the police at a warehouse. He was with the wiseguys, but he wasn't armed or anything. It was an accident, crossfire."

I took a minute or so with this. "Tell me more."

"Your father was a wonderful guy, would never hurt a flea. He grew up in the business, so it never occurred to him to get away from it, to try something else. But I don't think he was that comfortable with it. I think your father felt over his head. He hated having those crates of stuff around. Around you."

I realized at that moment for the first time, nobody buys that many cans of cranberry sauce. Or Frye boots. Or flatirons. ITSP, I thought involuntarily. Interstate Transportation of Stolen Property, 18 U.S. Code, Section 2314.

"Your father was with the wiseguys for business reasons, but his heart was with us. He was definitely one of the good guys. He was a source of information for us, for years. He even told us about the warehouse we raided the night he was—the night your father died."

"What cops were there?"

"A lot of people you know. Slifka, Domenic, Rudy."

"Who fired the shot?"

"There wasn't supposed to be any shooting at all. This kid on the wiseguy side panicked and emptied his Beretta in the general direction of the cops, and after that all hell broke loose, it was impossible to contain. We always thought the bullet your father stopped— I'm sorry, Terry—was from the wiseguy side, not the police side."

"You *thought?* You didn't *know?* Wasn't there even an *investigation*, for Christ's sweet sake?"

"It was kept quiet, Terry. Your father was our asset, they couldn't say they . . . that they, uh, removed their own asset. It would've been bad for the officers, it would've been bad for, for *you*, it would've hurt everybody. People were thinking about you. *I* was thinking about you."

"I know you were, Joe." I swallowed some of the stout. "I know you were. Always. And I'll never forget it. Thank you." I was crying freely.

Joe rose to go. I pulled myself together. "Joe, one more thing?" He sat back down.

"Sure, Terry."

"Operation Submarine?"

"Yes?" I could see already in his eyes that I was right.

"The case went together beautiful, it tried beauti-ful, never saw a case go in so fast. Seamless, like. Once you got immunity, you guys did a great job for us."

"Sure, right."

"Just one thing." I studied my beer murderously.

"Oh? What's that?"

"After the trials were all over, Tarzan figured out how our information was so good. He confronted me with it, and I 'fessed up."

"Been happening for years, Terry. I must've seen twenty of them myself."

"Not my point. Point is, after my meeting with Tarzan, I went back over all the confidential logs, all the wire material we never used. And I made a list of all the coded references on the tapes, and I made some charts, some new ones, not the ones you guys prepared for the trials."

"And?"

"There was another guy. There was a witness we never called, or even knew about. A high-ranking wit-ness."

Joe looked at me. Finally, without nodding or even moving his lips much, he said, "There was another guy."

"Who was it?"

"Solano."

"Jesus Christ, Rudy was in *that*? What *wasn't* he in?"

Joe said simply, "We couldn't have Rudy as a defendant in that case, Terry. Too . . . too complicated." He got up and this time left the bar without a back-ward glance. I was glad he did; there was no telling what I might see if I looked in his face again. So I was a mob brat! I stayed in the booth until 11:00 P.M., skipped dinner, and got dead drunk on Old Crow.

Needless to say, over the next several weeks I had to rearrange quite a bit of mental furniture to make room for what Joe had told me. And I couldn't share this labor with anyone: not with my Justice Department colleagues, not with my cop friends, certainly not with Rudy Solano. I decided I had been dealt a providential hand; this was a perfect time, almost a necessary time, to make a clean break and start a new life.

By the time I began work in Boston, I had my story straight. And no one in Boston knew enough background to cross-examine me about the soft spots.

A year and a half later, though, as the campaign for district attorney progressed, the press wanted to know more and more about me, about my background, about my work in New York. Since this meant free publicity, I had to pretend to welcome the scrutiny: I did three or four in-depth sit-down interviews a week. These put me under considerable pressure, as I had to be (and appear to be) forthcoming, while at the same time avoiding any statement that could be successfully contradicted. Worst of all, in several areas I could not turn to Lanny to help me shape the narrative. Joe Balls had been right: Because I had no one to confide in, I had no one to rely on but myself.

The good news, I guess, is that having to rely on yourself builds character.

chapter ten

Hens and Drakes

My overnight at the Quabbin with Emma had set the hook as deep in me as in the four-pound salmon. Campaigning is a full-time job, but it sure makes those twenty car rides a day easier if you can think about someone saline and sweet, refreshing and warming. I felt a foundation, a sturdiness, that was new to me. Opinions and answers came more naturally, though of course there was no logical connection between Emma and the DA's race. I was finally strutting on a wider stage, but because of her, I found I didn't have to act so much.

I knew I had only a limited amount of time. There are two campaigns in a major political race: before Labor Day, when no one is paying attention, and after Labor Day, when everyone is paying attention. I needed to see Emma during the summer.

It was not easy to arrange. I was a candidate for a highly visible elected public office in the most blood-sport-oriented political forum in America, and she was a married woman, even though many people in the Boston legal community didn't know it. Emma wore no ring.

In June, one of my ex-partners at W&C told me he was friends with a farmer in Orange, Massachusetts, who had too many pigeons in his barns and silo; would I consider joining him in a Saturday shoot? Emma agreed to accompany us, though she said she would not carry a gun.

That was the damnedest afternoon of blazing away I've ever had. The farmer wanted those birds *gone*, and he didn't care about birdshot on the inside of his barns or silo. We nearly melted the barrels of our 20-gauges, must have shot five or six boxes of shells apiece. I was glad I had only a recent vintage Franchi. Any Damascus steel, in a fine old gun like the Purdy I had bought in London, would have been ruined.

We were hunting to eat as well as to kill. We picked up every last bird, and plucked them, and I made a pigeon-and-rabbit cassoulet for eight at my ex-partner's house in Shrewsbury that night. His wife lost her appetite when the main course arrived, but Emma proved herself a real trencherwoman.

The only tense moment I had all day was when I walked out to the end of a field behind the main barn to find a bird I had seen go down, near the edge of the woods. It got up in the long grass ten yards from me and I put it down at twenty, a little close, but that wasn't the problem. The problem was that this pigeon's mate saw what had happened, and whizzed over and began flying in circles around the fallen corpse, emitting the most unpigeonlike shrieks. This was a bit rough. I looked back to the main barn, and beyond it noted Emma and two other women chatting by the cars. I didn't want to risk Emma seeing this little drama, so I quickly shot the shrieking pigeon dead. It fell within five feet of its mate. Even as a veteran hunter, I didn't feel great about that.

Later in the week, I came to Maple Ave. in Cambridge to collect Emma for an early dinner. I had duded myself up in wide-wale green corduroys, open tattersall shirt, light brown raw silk jacket, dark brown laced Peal's. Emma didn't even look up as I came in. She was deep in her beloved Nabokov, *Transparent Things.* "Transparent things, through which the past shines," said I knowledgeably. "Darkly," she grumbled.

"Would you like to know what that book reminds me of?"

"Yes, very much, because I remember Haberfeld's First Law: You Can't Discuss a Book Intelligently Until Before You've Read It."

"I've read it. What I think of is pondweeds."

"Oh, that's very nice, loved her, hated him. . . ."

"No, pondweeds, not The Pondweeds."

"You mean, they've put Captain Myosis and Lieutenant Mitosis on the job, and they still haven't been able to socialize pondweeds?"

"Afraid not. I guess there are some organisms destined to be always on the outside looking in, never wear the colors, never row at Henley, whatever. . . . You think the past influences the present?"

Emma looked up at me. "I think the past and the present are the same thing. What did you, *skip* Einstein in college, or something?"

"Ouch!" I said. "Listen, this isn't fair. I could barely follow the synopsis of the Unabomber's math thesis when the *New York Times* printed it."

"Lucky you," said Emma. She looked radiant, wrapped in the weeds of her own past. I could almost see them.

"You seem to have a certain amount of confidence in yourself. Does it come from all that time with birds and fish?"

"I do think so." She smiled and hugged her knees. "But—not to put too fine a point on it, of course—you, too. Where does yours come from?"

I felt a flush of embarrassment. "Oh, I've got a few birds, too."

"What kind?"

"Nuthatches," I blurted. Her eyes narrowed; she evidently saw this was forbidden ground. She turned to her book.

After a brief, uneasy spell, she was back: "Also, can I ask you something?"

Mother Mary, I said to myself. Sure, just as long as it has zero intellectual content. "Naturally, sweethead, fire away."

"Did you *enjoy* shooting that second bird that was circling around its mate?"

I had been seen! "Ohhh . . . You always hurt the one you love," I offered weakly. I was on the ropes.

Emma decided to let me regain my balance. "I suppose we shouldn't worry," she said, patting my hand, "since loving and dying are the same thing." I thought I saw mischief flit across her eyes. "In fact, loving and *killing* are the same thing. Don't try to tell me that catching a fish and shooting an animal aren't like scoring, for guys."

I felt, on behalf of all men everywhere, that an inner wall had been breached. The best defense might be a good offense. "Are you sure you're not a *Buddhist*? It's beginning to sound like *every* thing is the *same* thing. Aah-ooom . . ." I concluded ironically.

Now she took my hands, both of them. "Terry, there are lots of things that melt, or vanish, or die, as you achieve them or enjoy them. Not just fish and game. Think of a peach. Or a firecracker. Or those cave paintings in France, dripping away because of body heat from the tourists. Or the sight of a surprised bird. Think of ice cream! Or maybe"—she winked at me, *winked*, as though I was a three-year-old—"maybe even gaining a high public office!"

Ouch again. I moaned out loud.

Emma advanced on my position, my hopeless position. "You know what I like about you?"

This was a promising vein. "What you like about me? What you can't get enough of about me? No, what is it that drives you mad with desire about me?"

She giggled. "I didn't say that. What I like is you appear to be a man of many moods, but only one tense."

"Namely?"

"You live life in the present."

"Absolutely. If you look back, something might be gaining on you. Also, Lanny says I should."

"It's important to do what Lanny says." She leaned over. "It's also important to do what I say." She undid the third button on my shirt.

The DA race consumed me for most of the month, but Lanny gave me a Sunday lunch and afternoon off to spend with Emma. I rang the Maple Ave. doorbell smartly at noon-oh-one. The buzzer buzzed, no voice. Not Emma's usual modus operandi. I hurried up.

The apartment door was open. She was sitting by the window on a sofa, leafing through a picture album. Cushions and books had been tossed all over the floor. I put on a bright face and strode across to give her a kiss and look over her shoulder. When I was almost there she turned, and I stopped.

Emma's eyes were puffy and there were rutted tear tracks down her cheeks. She'd been at it for some time. Worse, the album was a folio of shots of her and Elijah Low: first in an academic group discussion, not noticing each other, then at a restaurant, with lots of other Chinese guys—the shy dawn of love, I thought sarcastically—finally, overt True Romance, wedding bells, travels in the Far East, then . . . nothing. The album stopped with Emma wearing fashions of four years ago.

"What's up?" I said, without giving her that kiss.

"Elijah's staying in Hong Kong," she said.

"What do you mean, he's staying in Hong Kong?" She seemed to catch herself. "Oh, it's not really that big a deal, actually. It's just that he's decided, he's decided, for business reasons, he needs to be there this summer, for the rest of this summer, so he's just going to, ah, remain on site." She gave me a defensive look. "It's not like he's *hiding out* or anything, he's going to be at the *Mandarin*, they do have telephones. . . ."

Telephones, I thought. Great.

"And . . . there's something else."

Although I knew in my bones what was coming, I asked, "Oh? What's that?"

Emma slumped, then forced it out: "Elijah is insisting I join him in Hong Kong in September. Permanently. He says his family insists on it, too."

I froze. Elijah Low, who would screw a cat in business, who would saw a man in half, was going to take my Emma world away from me. A not unfamiliar refrain pounded through my temples. *Tough for the kid tough for the kid tough* . . . I couldn't let Emma see. I walked in a circle, keeping my back to her. I pressed my temple with the heel of my hand.

"Emma, sweetheart, I can see you're . . . you're busy, on the busy side. Howbout I give you a ring tomorrow—tomorrow afternoon—and we talk about maybe getting together for lunch or coffee this week."

"That'd be lovely," she said. The tears had started again. I closed the door behind me without a word or a sound. I had not felt this sense of violation in many years, but I remembered it vividly. I kept it to myself, since I had no other options, and in the short term plunged back into the work of the campaign.

*   *   *

That Thursday Rudy Solano was up in Boston with his buddies Fay and St. Onge because the National District Attorneys' Association was having their annual convocation at the Park Plaza. Just what I needed: a nationwide forum for the views of the host DA, the Honorable Martin Gross.

Gross had good play in the local media on the opening day extravaganza, but, strangely, his press operation seemed to lack follow-through and the story ran out of legs. For day two's news, I persuaded the state auditor, who was a pal of mine, to make a major announcement challenging the legal authority of Governor Lovett to privatize the state mass transit workers, as he was endeavoring to do. This was red meat for the press, this was functionally Irish versus Yankee, even though the state auditor was an Armenian. Never let the facts get in the way of a good story, as the best reporters say.

The headline from my point of view—or, rather, lack of headline—was that Martin Gross's day in the limelight remained a day, not two days or more. The town was preoccupied with the howitzer blasts between Lovett and Kasparian. We couldn't get in the Gross story directly—nobody would've printed a word we said—so using Kasparian as a beard was our only recourse. Nice carom shot, said Lanny, who was finishing most days over the felt at Jillian's or Boston Billiards. Knight move, I replied.

Rudy stayed in town an extra day after the convention to catch up with me. We went to have a beer at the Golden Badge, an unmarked Boston police watering hole in Hyde Park. Both patrolmen and superior officers were welcome, but nobody who was not family, i.e., police and guests only. Rudy had access through Fay and St. Onge. He led me to the ground-floor bar, which was staffed but thinly patronized. Plenty of privacy here, even if not much elegance. It reminded me of the On Leong clubhouse in Brooklyn, to tell you the truth. Through the plywood walls, I could hear other nail-booted arrivals tramping up a set of stairs. There were rooms on the second and third floors where the officers could relax.

Rudy asked how the campaign was going.

"Real good, Rudy. I think Fay and St. Onge may be able to deliver the big one, if we can hold our own on the macro-front, on the airwaves."

"Howbout you, Terry? How you doin'? How you doin' financially? How you doin' in the market?"

"I'm not doing anything financially. I mean, I'm doing fine. Who wants to know, anyway?"

"Nobody wants to know, nobody wants to know. I was just curious, is all. Howbout personally?"

I told him about Emma. I told him about Emma and me. Then I told him about Elijah Low.

"He sounds like a real peach," said Rudy. "He's never here, he wants to send for her? Like, he doesn't want to attend the Academy Awards, he says, 'Just ship me the Oscar'? What's he do for a living?"

"Emma met him when he was an adjunct professor at her law school, teaching international business stuff. But when I asked her what was his business in Hong Kong that kept him away so much, she laughed and said, 'Organized crime.' She said it like she was joking, but she also said he would screw a cat in business, so I don't know." I studied the bubbles in my Pauli Girl. "I wouldn't mind knowing a little more about him."

Rudy gave a low whistle. "I wonder if any of our old friends might know a thing or two about him."

"That's what I was just thinking."

"I could call the Royals." This meant the Hong Kong Royal Police.

"No, don't call the Royals, that's too overt, might get back to him."

"I could use the other channel," said Rudy. "My relationships there are even stronger, so that should be a piece of cake." He laughed.

"I don't know," I said vaguely.

"Sure, I know you don't," Rudy replied. There was something in his tone I didn't appreciate, perhaps a hint of sarcasm. I decided to let it ride.

"He's staying at the Mandarin until September."

"Got it. You can't do better than that."

We paid our tab and Rudy hopped a cab for Logan. We shook hands.

"See you in church," said Rudy.

"See you in church," I replied. This was a running joke between us. Neither of us took in more than a mass or two a month.

Rudy called me a few days later from New York. At home.

"I, uh, got in touch with an old friend. That report about the individual we were discussing checks out positive. That is to say, negative. Bad guy."

"What kind?"

"Aliens, some narcotics. Mainly Thailand, Laos. Hong Kong travel agency front. Classic."

"What about the professor thing?"

"Huge front, great front, lots of travel. Very interested in business laws of Hong Kong, Laos, Burma, Thailand. Of course, they don't have any, so I assume he's still looking. But he's well and truly holed up at the Mandarin. He's not lacking for, uh, pleasant company around town, either."

"So he wants it both ways, with Emma. The hell with him, I mean the hell with that."

"I'll see you in church, Boss." Rudy hung up before I could process his unwelcome news any further.

chapter eleven

Running as an Underdog

The truth is, we should have lost the race for district attorney. On paper, I had virtually nothing going for me. Martin Gross was a well-respected eleven-year incumbent who had been a state rep from the vote-rich wards of Dorchester for ten years prior to that. I was a blow-in from the hated Big Apple, home of the Rangers and the Knicks and, worst of all, the Yankees. Bucky Dent's 1978 home run in the one-game playoff still rankled in sports bars and parlors all over the city.

But because I had nothing, I had nothing to lose. Furthermore, although I was intrigued by the unions' offer of a stealth organization and I did think Gross had a few miles on him, I did not expect to win and so I was not worried about losing.

Both of these circumstances made me an extremely dangerous candidate, in retrospect.

Our command staff was slim and the payroll was slimmer.

Lanny Green as campaign manager worked for

virtually nothing, putting in twenty-hour days. He bummed a room off a Washington friend, a Nigerian, who had an apartment in Bay Village. For food, I think the AFL-CIO must have sent him CARE packages. Lanny's major expenditure appeared to be Camels: he smoked incessantly. Not filters, either. I love to see people smoke nonfilter cigarettes, the same way I love to see them reading *Vogue* or *Popular Mechanics* or racing car magazines. It means the people are doing what they want to do, instead of listening to someone else tell them what they should do. Emma is right, I do live in the present. Anyway, the harder Lanny worked, the more charged up he got. Most people are like that.

Lanny hired Jerry Traugott, a *Daily Mail* style section reporter with cascading ringlets of dark hair, to come on board as press secretary. I was mystified. "Lanny, she covers *fashion*," I protested.

Lanny was cool. "We're not looking for substantive knowledge, Boss. We, or rather you, already have that, or we wouldn't be in this thing in the first place. The point is, everybody in town knows Jerry, everybody in town likes Jerry, nobody in town is threatened by Jerry, because they think she's a bubblehead on account of she just goes to shows and parties and writes about them. But she is not. She is very smart. Trust me, Boss, she'll do fine."

With just an occasional suggestion from Lanny, Jerry Traugott did do fine. We had a bit of a bump in the road early on, when a senior *Daily Mail* opinion writer she was bedding down with wrote a thumb-sucker for the Sunday paper wondering out loud about my qualifications for the job. But Lanny had it pegged just right: underneath it all, even just underneath the Laura Ashleys, fashion and gossip reporters are always good for an icepick to the heart. She cut the guy off immediately, breaking a date to go to the Celtics game, and then back to her place, that very night. She declined to take his increasingly frantic calls thereafter, at home or at work.

After that, seldom was heard a discouraging word from Jerry's many friends in the business. Because they didn't view her as a threat, they wanted her to succeed. Many of the reporters seemed more interested in trashing the seven candidates in the primaries for the statewide races. Like Lanny, Jerry was working twenty-hour days.

We didn't pay anybody for field. Lanny was insistent—manic, really—that having paid people on staff dries up the enthusiasm of your volunteers, and by the end of the race I was sure he was right. Gross had a paid field staff of eight, and maybe thirteen volunteers, while we had a paid field staff of zero and three hundred regulars. We needed that war room at 99½ State Street.

Lanny set up a "Truth Squad," a twenty-four-hour-a-day rapid response team of volunteer researchers, mostly college kids, whose job was to rebut any unfavorable allegation or story *in the same news trough*, so the media would at a minimum have to include our side of the beef. More often, our fact checkers were able to bat down rumors or negative stories before they even ran. That's assuming the reporters were serious about running them in the first place: there's a lot of "testing" that goes on in the news coverage of political campaigns. Reporters like to drop a penny in the well and listen for the echo or splash, to see how deep the candidate's well is and what it has in it.

The law enforcement "issues" I didn't need any help with, and the police union guys, Fay and St. Onge, helped us with the delicate questions of where the bodies were buried in various investigations and court cases.

All in all, it was a lovely, lean machine.

Gross got handed an extremely hot potato early on when a couple of prostitutes who were hauled into Boston Municipal Court for the Monday-morning session complained they shouldn't be there, because they had paid their "dues" at the Golden Badge, the Hyde Park police club, on the way to jail on Saturday. These ladies were not first-timers in the BMC, which ordinarily would have undercut their credibility, but Judge Donham seemed quite interested in their testimony that a prostitute could be "unarrested" by certain officers for the price of two hours' dalliance upstairs at the Golden Badge. Custom of the street, they said unaffectedly, as though surely everyone knew that. They were laughing. They weren't really complaining, just explaining. Goes to show you shouldn't do either. They said this officer who was a particular friend of theirs had gotten drunk and gone home to his wife, and the duty sergeant who then came across them was not in on the game. So they got no credit. All they wanted was what they were entitled to. They didn't take any of this seriously.

When Judge Donham asked them to describe the rooms on the third floor of the Golden Badge, they realized he *did* take their story seriously. They also noticed that the judge had taken over the questioning, and that the assistant district attorney had gotten very quiet.

They looked around the courtroom and saw a few familiar faces. Plain clothes, but familiar faces. Not smiling faces.

At that point, the two ladies said they could not describe the third floor of the Golden Badge, and became evasive about all aspects of the story they had blurted out. That left the judge with nowhere to go, but the police reporter from the *Daily Mail* was not bound by their recantation, and he wrote up a pretty good sidebar on their testimony.

Everybody in town wanted to know what Martin Gross was going to do about it. He was between a rock and a hard place: legally, he didn't have any evidence, but many people believed the prostitutes' original story anyway. Like me, for example.

Lanny asked me what I would do if I were DA. I said I would immunize everybody, throw them in the grand jury one by one, threaten everybody with perjury if their story didn't hold up or contempt if they dummied up, and wait for the first crack.

Lanny winced. "There goes the field organization. This ain't like talking about what you did to somebody else in New York years ago, this would hit them where they eat."

"Eat?"

"Gimme a break, Boss."

"Well, if you want to duck it, I could say I can't comment on a pending investigation. That was always our rule in New York: we never comment on pending investigations—unless we want to."

"Sounds good."

District Attorney Gross, however, had no such luxury. As the incumbent, he had to face the question whether there was an investigation, and if not, why not?

In truth, the only way to have gotten to the bottom of the mess was the course I outlined to Lanny, but Gross didn't have the nerve for open war with the police, especially as the two witnesses were now denying everything they had said. So he closed it out with no charges, and rightly suffered a major black eye with the media for doing so.

Sometimes, I concluded, it's *better* to be on the outside looking in.

Lanny and Jerry leaked to the press, on a not-for-attribution basis, anything we could find out about pending investigations or even just plain dirty laundry. Not a single reporter ever blew our cover for us. I love the working press. And it's not an oxymoron, as some wags suggest. I tell whoever will listen that of all the people in public office, prosecutors probably like the press the most, because we're all trying to knock down the same temple walls.

The last guy who was in all the campaign meetings was Nestor "Bull" Flannery, a beefy Charlestown homie who had been a sportswriter for the *Gazette* for over thirty years and was now retired. Bull's assignment was to Bostonize me. In one of our first meetings, I made the mistake of saying "between you and me," and he was off on a tear. "Boy, you really are a blow-in, kid, ain't you?" he said sharply. "Now, listen up, and listen good: in Boston, it's 'between you and I,' and don't you ever forget it."

The Sisters of Charity would have groaned if they could have heard me, but I became a willing and frequent solecist under Flannery's tutelage. After one rap on the knuckles, I could click off "So isn't Murphy!"—meaning, so *is* Murphy—like a native. *Dic, duc, fer, fac.* When in Rome.

All of these people loved the game, and the morale at headquarters was good, to put it mildly. Lanny and Jerry and I—excuse me, Lanny and Jerry and me—often played hearts at HQ while waiting for the ten o'clock and eleven o'clock news, and we developed a currency to separate the winners from the losers. Top winner got to designate any English word of his or her choosing, and loser had to use it in conversation within the next twenty-four hours, while dealing with the press. An out-of-town reporter actually complained to Jerry when, after a rum run of luck, I used "oxter" and "syzygy" on consecutive days. Jerry explained that I had gone to parochial school in Brooklyn and the reporter said, "Oh! Sorry!" and dropped it.

A more sophisticated variant of this penalty was unwittingly suggested by Bull Flannery, who was the most prolific generator of malapropisms and mixed metaphors I have ever encountered. "You can really hear the handwriting on the wall on this one," he would say, or "Let's not deprave them of the opportunity to shoot themselves in the foot," or "He's the splitting image of Cardinal Cushing," or, worse, "You're just spitting hairs." So, in time, the penalty for taking the queen of spades too often was to use a hideous and garish mixed metaphor suggested by the winning party. (Flannery wasn't a player in this game, just a "founder.") My favorite was dreamed up by Jerry Traugott, who pinned it on the luckless Lanny just before an on-the-record session with the *Gazette* ed board: "And then, the hand of fate stepped in." Lanny said it very quickly at the end of a pointless story, hoping no one would notice, but the editor of the *Gazette* editorial page, a brainy lady and one of the few people in town whose opinion meant something to Lanny, howled out loud and never let him forget it. He refused to play hearts with us for almost a month.

Lanny never scheduled our morning staff meeting until 9:30 A.M., to accommodate his own and Jerry's night owl ways. But he was always crisp and he spent as many hours stroking the press on the telephone as Jerry did.

He never missed a beat. Play 'em like you got 'em was his motto and mine. Act like you own the joint, even if you don't. Lanny played a lot of poker, and a lot of billiards. Not pool, that was too straightforward. Three-cushion billiards. The carom is not a by-product of the shot, the carom is the shot.

"Yes, we know all about it, Howard, thanks for

calling, complete tragedy, breakdown in the system, off-the-record Gross should have been all over this family like a cheap suit six months ago at the first sign of trouble. . . . No, that was off the record. No, we don't have any comment at this time, we'll do a noon avail on scene, catch us live, real tears, we care, be there or be square. . . ."

Jerry yawned and stretched. "Our metropolis has not had a good beginning to its day, is that it?"

"There's some ugly situation out in Mattapan, one kid dead, dysfunctional family, crack addict mother. I blamed Gross OTR."

"What's the case about?"

"I actually had never heard of it," Lanny admitted. "Must of missed it on the radio this morning, water running or something, happens alla time. Anyhooo, we are now committed to doing a full media availability, in Mattapan at noon precisely, so, Nestor, you better find out what this case is about. Anytime between now and five minutes from now would be great. Call Fay, why don't you."

The phone rang again. One of our volunteer receptionists swelled with pride and put it through. A freckle-faced blonde, she looked about fourteen, but I was assured she was old enough to attend the office beer and pizza parties. Which meant, I later learned, that she had to be at least fifteen, which she cleared by three months. In political campaigns, youth must serve and be served. President Kennedy had it at least half right.

"Lanny Green. Yeh, Randy. No, not at all. Well, as

a matter of conscience, Terry is against abortion, so I guess you could say in that sense he's prolife." I began waving my hands in front of Lanny's face. "But only in that sense. Anyway, he's going to enforce the law, whatever the law may be from time to time, so it's really not an issue in this race. Oh, yes, Terry's a law man all the way." Lanny hung up.

"Randy Curran. *Ledger*. Trying to nail us on the abortion issue for his suburban soccer moms. I could care less for this race, he doesn't have three readers who vote in Suffolk, but I don't like this for future—"

Here I broke in. "Lanny, how about we salami it on abortion, we're actually prochoice, but troubled by taxpayer funding, that sort of thing?"

"Oh, that's good, Terry. Very good idea, particularly given what we've already said. Terry, that would be like if England switched from driving on the left side of the road to the right side *in stages*—trucks this week, buses next week, then foreign cars, last but not least the few surviving Morris Minors. . . ."

Lanny suddenly frowned and his voice and body both swiveled in midphrase. "Hey, Jerry, back to that noon avail? On second thought, bad photo op, we could be accused of hotdogging, et cetera. Hell, we could even be accused of not knowing what we're talking about, outrageous as that would be. Can you get on the horn and move the noon live to a four P.M. press conference, Stanbro Room, Park Plaza? Tell them we'll read something, probably no questions—no, they won't buy that, um, no other topics. Limited focus. The City Hall guys will rightly be too lazy to cover that, and I think I'd rather be out of this story than in it. We can put out a boring release. Make it so boring it's unusable."

Jerry executed this assignment to perfection, and carefully put Lanny's name on the release as the press contact, rather than her own. He didn't care whether people thought he was a lousy writer, she did.

The next call was for Jerry, guy trying to snooker confidential polling information out of her. She put on a mock falsetto: "Stuart Cross, you big snake, you. Don't you know I'm too smart to succumb to your blandishments? Oh, no, I'd walk a *mile* to avoid a scene, you know I really would." She batted her eyes at the receiver. First telephone sex, now telephone foreplay, I thought to myself. What won't they come up with next?

"I'd love to, Stuart," Jerry was cooing into the phone. "How about December? Does December work for you? Noo? Well, then, how about never—does never work? Ohh, you're more than sweet to say so, but I'm afraid I've got to run now, my toast just popped up." She pushed the "off" button as though it were a detonator.

Lanny turned to Jerry. "Don't you love guys like Stuart Cross?"

"Can't get enough of them," said Jerry. "First he's frustrated because he's a lousy reporter, so he's developed a mean streak as broad as his back. Second, he's a stranger to the truth. He always says he's returning your call, even when nobody called him. Third, he's so dumb he wouldn't know if you cut his throat 'til he turned to laugh at you and his head fell off."

The icepick was certainly not getting rusty.

*   *   *

Lanny was right, the media did not cover our press conference, and we were not in the story the next day. Who *was* in the story the next day was Gross, engaging in a virtual screaming match with three TV reporters and Andy Toshay, the WARQ radio anchor, over why these children hadn't been removed from their crack-head mother months before. After explaining for the third time that he really wasn't the goddamn Department of Social Services, Gross finally lost his cool and committed the unforgivable sin of suggesting that one of the TV reporters didn't know what he was talking about. This rallied every other news outlet in the city to the defense of the reporter, who, in fact, had had absolutely no idea what he was talking about.

In the day-one follow stories, Lanny limited our role to basically "tsk, tsk." But when the feud between Gross and the TV people turned into a shooting war on day two, with mutual accusations of incompetence, Lanny decided to jump in. This time, we did do a noon live shot, not for the top of the hour, but for twelve minutes in, when the background footage of the screaming match would already have aired.

Lanny instructed me to say that I didn't under-stand what the dispute was about, because if it had not been for the investigative work by the TV reporters, these deplorable conditions in Mattapan would never have been discovered; indeed, in a way, the reporters were doing the job that should have been done by *public safety officials*—I was to put on my most lugubrious face here—and if more had been done earlier, these human tragedies might have been averted. Simple and straightforward. Just took us a three-hour prep session to cook it up.

Beset by my training as a prosecutor, I suffered a burst of candor. "Lanny, that's flat-out not true. The TV reporters didn't do jack-all. The only reason they showed up is because the kid was dead."

Lanny stubbed out his cigarette and exhaled slowly. "Terry, let me break this down. The question for us is not what is true. The courts will sort that out in the fullness of time, through criminal trials and procedures too numberless for me even to contemplate, not that I would want to. If I had wanted to, I would have gone to law school. The question for *us* is what are Channels Four, Five, and Seven going to show on the noon news? And the answer is, whatever you say, as long as you back up their version of events. As for the newspapers, they can print only what you say, if they play it straight. And I think they will play this one straight, straight between Gross's shoulder blades, because they're smelling a little blood."

I buried my head in my hands. "Just let me ask you folks one question." I looked up and around. I was not in a good mood. "Is this all on the level?"

Bull Flannery looked at me with scorn, Lanny with compassion. It was Flannery who spoke.

"Nothing's on the level, kid."

I realized they were telling me the time had come to teach it flat. And when the time came, I delivered my lines like a champ, if I do say so myself.

chapter twelve

The Roller Coaster

Labor Day weekend was a love-in, particularly the AFL-CIO breakfast at the Park Plaza, which Lanny and the police union guys had completely wired for me. The emcee told all the legislators in the audience if they had a 100 percent AFL-CIO voting record, next year they could be up on the dais. Such a deal! You get to spend five hours there instead of two!

Gross left after half an hour—significant mistake—and the council then went back into its business session and considered an item not on the printed agenda, namely, the question of an endorsement for district attorney of Suffolk County. Guess what? It was unanimous. That was worth a lot of signs, a lot of bumper stickers, and a lot of legs.

I was feeling great about the world as I sailed into the headquarters Tuesday morning around nine-thirty. My two breakfast fund-raisers had exceeded projections by 75 percent. Not big absolute dollars yet, but a promising sign.

Our proud young receptionist said a messenger had left an envelope for me. She didn't have quite her usual smile. She handed me the envelope. The return address was Emma's law firm, Rankin and Shaw, but the handwritten initials were "H. N." I opened the envelope. It was a copy of a telegram, dated the previous Friday. After a few words, I felt the hammer going to work in my temples.

The telegram was from the Royal Hong Kong Police Department. It explained that one Elijah Low, the husband of Ms. E. Gallaudette, had been found dead in his car, a badly smashed-up BMW. Worse, he was in the company of a young Chinese woman, also dead, and there were indications that the woman was a prostitute and that liquor had been very much a factor in the accident. The telegram hadn't even come directly to Emma; it had been delivered to the managing partner of the firm, Howard Nerman. The allosaurus.

Emma was in Houston for a real estate negotiation and closing, had been there for ten days. I called at once and told her how sorry I was for her sake. Her voice, while clearly not normal, sounded more tired and resigned than heartbroken. I asked her if she would like me to find out any further details I could from her managing partner, whom I knew she despised. She said yes and actually thanked me. Thanked *me*, who was waiting to be struck dead because I was filled with joy that Emma seemed more resigned than distraught!

Nerman answered his own phone on the first ring.

I explained I was a close friend of Emma and her late husband—he said, "Yes, I know!"—and said Emma had asked me to find out if there were any legal proceedings in Hong Kong, other than the funeral arrangements, or any other details of which she should be aware.

Nerman spoke quickly and distinctly: "I anticipated that. I've already faxed a series of questions to the Royal Hong Kong Police. I have their response, in writing. There is no pending legal investigation. The case is closed. The ruling is accidental death. There will be no charges, criminal or civil, against anyone. The police have no questions for Mrs. Low, that is, Ms. Gallaudette. I have also been in touch with Mr. Low's family. The funeral mass, in case Ms. Gallaudette has not yet received word, will be performed in Hong Kong next Thursday. I have arranged for another partner to relieve Ms. Gallaudette from her responsibilities for the matter in Houston, effective immediately. Is there anything else?"

"Thank you, sir," I said, and pressed the "off" button. I couldn't wait the one second it would take to hang up. No wonder Emma can't stand him, I thought: he obviously can't wait to get back to stealing cases from other lawyers in the firm.

Emma left for Hong Kong, alone, directly from Houston. The whole episode was surreal to me. I felt nothing for Elijah Low, but I knew at one point Emma had thought enough of him to marry him. I knew I would not believe he was gone until I saw Emma again. Alone.

*   *   *

Because the September 17 primary against Martin Gross was almost upon us, I had no time whatsoever to dwell on Elijah's death, or even my possible future with Emma. There are no Republicans to speak of in Boston or Suffolk County, so the Democratic primary is tantamount to election. Lanny forbade me even to call Hong Kong, once I confirmed that Emma had arrived safely.

"Boss, I'm sorry about Emma's loss, but we're twelve days out, and we can't afford to have one ounce of energy or one nickel left over after the third Tuesday in September. If we do, we'll kick ourselves all the way back to your law office—where you'll be spending the next four years. This is no marathon now, this is a sprint. Don't even take time out to brush your teeth. Well, you can brush, but don't floss."

I didn't floss, and I didn't call Emma, and I stayed on message. A week before the primary, Lanny took me to sit with the *Daily Mail* editorial board. This and a session the next day with Gross would likely decide their endorsement.

Lanny and I sat in the back as Rye Kooch drove us over, and I was nervous for the first time in I don't know how long. I was making some notes and my right hand was shaking. "This isn't even funny," I said grimly. My hands never shake. I've been hunting deer since I was sixteen years old, and as I told you, I've never once gotten buck fever.

Lanny was as cool as though we were all sitting around the Oval Office. Nothing bad could happen in the political realm as long as you were talking to Lanny, you felt. "Time to come out of the crouch, Boss," he said. "If we pour it on now, they'll just print what we say, they won't haggle the way they've been doing. This is show time, this is the play-offs, and the refs are going to let us play. The reason you feel antsy is you're a trial guy underneath it all, you're taught to go for the jugular, and we've been holding you in check. Now is the time to play hit and run, believe me, and not stand around arguing about how much blood there was."

I felt a rush. "Fine with me," I said, and noticed that my hand had stopped shaking. Lanny saw, too. "You've got the nerve of a burglar," he said admiringly.

"Some things you don't joke about," I suggested. Lanny burst into loud, uncharacteristic laughter.

Despite its importance, the meeting with the *Daily Mail* ed board was an anticlimax, since I was reciting my lines. That was one thing I knew how to do.

Why did I want to be district attorney in Boston? Bingo. "Because of the state we're in, in both senses of the word. This is no time for a lowering of voices; this is no time for a period of benign neglect. I'm worried about the corrosion of our institutions. I'm worried about the undermining of public confidence in our court system and even in our democracy.

"I know some people say that corruption doesn't hurt anybody. That's nonsense! That's"—here I took a breath—"balderdash!" I snuck a quick peek around and saw that my daring choice of words had met with bow-tied approval. I thought, What the heck, I'll have a little fun.

"An attitude like that makes our job impossible. A witness who doesn't think bribery or extortion is a serious crime is never going to come forward. A prosecutor who is reluctant to challenge ingrained habits is part of the problem, not part of the solution.

"I'll tell you one thing. If I get in there, I'm going to hit the ground running. I'm going to surround myself with bright young lawyers from the best blue-chip firms in Boston"—this met with *strong* bow-tied approval—"and tell them I want them to develop complex, high-impact cases, as I did in Brooklyn, that *would not be brought if we didn't work there.* I want the motto of the office to be: '*Attack* the power structure!' not '*Hide* from it!'"

I decided to go for the gold. "I'm worried if we countenance a public perception that the system is corrupt or rigged, you'll get the political equivalent of Gresham's law, where the bad players will drive the good players out of the game. That's not the Boston I want to see."

Enter my straight man, or rather woman. "Gresham's law??? Whaaaa?" whined Addie Stephens, a young, intelligent, up-from-the-streets reporter who seemed to have taken a scunner to me.

I would have loved to know what was the stick across her back, but in any case, this was an error on her part. "Oh, Addie, I think we all know what Gresham's theorem is," huffed the publisher, W. Bradford Parmelee.

"It's a monetary thing; you know: silver drives out gold, cheap drives out better. Remember William Jennings Bryan?" Stephens had no choice but to nod, as if to say, "Of course."

I damn well did remember William Jennings Bryan, and the Cross of Gold speech. I also remembered that the most vivid illustration of Gresham's law in twentieth-century America is not monetary currency at all but the mass media, where the bad news always drives out the good. I judged it best to keep this wise thought to myself, though, so as not to create bad news and step on my own story.

Addie Stephens made one more run at me. "Don't you think that Marty Gross has been doing all of that, at least in his second and third terms?"

I didn't hesitate. "There's been a certain amount of noise, I'll warrant you, particularly around election time. But with all deference, Martin Gross has been district attorney of this county for eleven and a half years, and I was a poor, broken-down, run-of-the-mill assistant U.S. attorney in New York for seven years, and I've personally convicted three times as many public officials as his entire office *ever* has." No one said anything. Stephens could only nod, again. I didn't even look around the room. I knew I had pierced this innermost citadel of Harvard with my snobby little arrow of Erudition. While you can never be sure, I felt I had been Accepted.

This time, I was right. Three days after our visit, the *Daily Mail* endorsed me in the primary. The

Gazette stayed with Gross, but their circulation was less than half that of the *Daily Mail*.

Gross fought back gamely over the last weekend, holding huge outdoor rallies in the Adams Hill section of Dorchester and on Hanover Street in the North End, but he couldn't overcome the *Daily Mail* endorsement: a hundred thousand "goo-goo"—good government—votes moved into my column on cue. We won by five and a half points.

In the Republican primary, a kid named Philip Vacco from Ward 3 ran unopposed. He was a presentable guy and by all accounts a pretty good lawyer—Notes and Comment editor on *BU Law Review*—but most people thought he was running for exercise, or to help his already successful law practice. He came from a political family but had never been a prosecutor, even.

The mood in our headquarters on primary night was consequently one of great hilarity. Everybody, myself included, felt that we had fought the good fight and won. And that it was now all over.

Everybody, that is, except Lanny, who hustled me into the back room.

"Lose the Budweiser, Boss, Four, Five, and Seven will be here at eight sharp for reaction, they'll call it as soon as the polls close. They can't call the statewides yet, too close, so we'll be first up. And get your game face back on."

"Why? Are we supposed to be afraid of Vacco? He's a Republican, and he's younger than I am!"

"Yeah, and we were ten points ahead of Gross with

three days to go, and we won by five. We lost ground on the street, not the airwaves, Boss. Something's wrong out there."

"But Vacco won't have anything going on the street."

"Point is, we lose ground when the media's with us, what's going to happen when the media turns?"

"What's going to make it turn?"

"Nothing. It just always does. They like horse races. What I want is to fast-forward to the election. Be boring. No stories, no attention between now and then."

For several weeks in September and October, I was running better than thirty points ahead of Phil Vacco, and it appeared that Lanny's worry had not been well founded. Then on Sunday, October 20, the *Daily Mail* ran a page-one Addie Stephens piece claiming that two independent sources within the Brooklyn U.S. attorney's office had told her I was ousted from the office for exceeding my authority in immunizing witnesses, and for concealing from my superiors the existence of an illegal wiretap during Operation Submarine.

Talk about an icepick to the heart. This story would take care of our thirty-point lead in a hurry unless we could blow it out of the water. Voters may form impressions early on, but, unlike officeholders, they tend not to get set in their ways, and they pay attention like hell the last two weeks.

The kids on our Truth Squad, much as they wanted to help and much as I loved them, were useless because there were no recorded facts to check here: in Brooklyn, this had all been handled orally and behind closed doors, because it was in everybody's interest to do so.

We held an emergency damage-control meeting of the senior staff, so I could get their sense of how the ground lay. Lanny seemed off his pins somewhat. He suggested that perhaps the whole dispute could be laid down to a misunderstanding, or a difference of opinion among attorneys.

For once, I elbowed Lanny aside. "Bullshit. There's only one way you can fight this kind of fire. And that's with bigger rounds going right back at them. If we try to waffle through this one, the whispers will kill me." No middle ground on this one, I said. I said I would call in the cops—meaning Luis Garcia and John Casey.

It was a short call. Yes, Garcia and Casey were happy to help. No, they did not need their recollections refreshed, they remembered everything vividly. Yes, they saw it my way. Yes, they could spare the time to come to Boston so the lions could eyeball and cross-examine them.

Okay, no further questions; your witnesses, Counsel!

The two of them held a joint news conference outside Boston Police Headquarters on Berkeley Street eight days before the election. They were attached to the office in New York at the time, they said, they knew everything that happened in that case, Terry Mullally made the case, Terry Mullally convicted the bad cops,

Terry Mullally purified the department, anyone who told it differently was just plain jealous. Or corrupt.

They were both magnificent. Give me a deer hunter every time, I thought. And still think.

Nobody in the Brooklyn U.S. attorney's office or the NYPD would say anything on the record to go against Casey and Garcia, and Burroughs, now a federal circuit judge, was out of the play. The TVs bought it. The *Gazette* bought it. And the *Daily Mail* retreated into a muddle.

On Election Day, November 5, we won by sixteen points. Our victory suite at the Park Plaza was packed with jubilant campaign workers. In the back room, Lanny was shaking his head.

"What's up," I said without sympathy.

"Forty-two percent. The guy's thirty-one years old, he's a Republican in Suffolk County, and he gets forty-two percent. He should have gotten four point two percent."

This was a virus I didn't want loose, not in that crowd, not that night.

"Lanny, for once relax. Nothing we can do about it now. Place is crawling with TV out there. Tonight we need the bright face, not the game face. We won. Oh, congratulations, incidentally."

Lanny remained sprawled in his chair.

"The guy's a good guy, Lanny, and not all that bad a candidate, and people aren't stupid, they can see that."

"The guy's a *Republican* guy."

"Lanny, Republicans are people, too."

"No, they're not."

"And he's *from* Boston, which I'm not, and he has a helluva political wife who can campaign for him, which I don't, and his uncle's a judge, which I don't have an uncle so mine's not, and he's Italian, which I'm not."

My patient brightened a little. "You think that was part of it?"

"I'm certain of it. Plus, I know how we can co-opt his base: Bring him into the office at a senior level. He'd kill for the trial experience. I've talked with him onstage before and after our debates. It would show mutual respect. A good thing. Never know where your next coalition is coming from."

Lanny was on his feet. "That's thinking like a pro, Boss. Let's go. Lotta TV out there."

Two days later, I received a telegram from Hong Kong:

I AM PROUD OF YOU AND I LOVE YOU.

Came right to the point. I like that. Saves time.

I was looking forward to seeing Emma rather more than I was to taking office. The campaign had been a series of nice steep learning curves for me, but I already knew how a prosecutor's office worked. Or, at least, should work.

chapter thirteen

Locke-Ober's Café

Emma returned from Hong Kong two weeks after the election in time for a quiet birthday dinner alone with me on November 22. I let her do the talking.

Her carriage was perfect. She didn't pretend she had never been married, she didn't pretend she had never loved Elijah, but equally she didn't pretend her marriage had been anything other than loveless since Elijah's fixation on his "business" ventures in the Far East. She said he had become a completely different person from the sympathetic teacher she had fallen for as a law student.

"The whole trip was eerie," Emma said over oysters Rockefeller in the small third-floor room at Locke-Ober's Café on Winter Place. Cozy, seats either two or four. Dark paneling, an opaque window with a diagonal crosshatch of lead mullions, straight out of medieval Germany. As a matter of fact, the whole restaurant is pretty much straight out of medieval Germany. That's why I love it so.

"Have you ever taken that flight?" Emma asked. "From Vancouver to Hong Kong, the plane is fleeing the dawn the whole way—just an hour ahead of the light. I felt as though I were fleeing everything, even though I was only doing what I was supposed to do. I dreamt that the captain came back to tell me it could be dawn if I wanted, and I told him to hold off on dawn until Elijah was buried and I was back in the United States."

"With anyone in particular?"

"With you, actually. You made a cameo appearance."

"I'm glad."

"I guess the circumstances of Elijah's death shed a little light on his business dealings, in social circles at least, because his family's attitude toward me was totally changed, for the better. They were most embarrassed and apologetic about everything, went out of their way for me, not a whisper of why hadn't the round-eye been cleaving herself to her mate in the East—which there had been a good deal of, in the past."

"You were there almost two months. We missed you."

Emma was distinctly dry-eyed about this cry from the heart. "I had to sign a lot of stuff for the lawyers, for his estate, and I wanted to get as much of it done over there as I could. I don't believe in long-distance lawyering. After that, I found I just couldn't face coming right back and going to work again for Howard Nerman, who I thought was probably eagerly waiting to send me to Dallas or Anchorage for six months on another negotiation. So I stayed for a few weeks with some British friends who live in Midlevels, sort of halfway up the Peak. It's a big expat community, lots of nationalities, not just England."

"Expat?"

"Expatriate."

"Learn something every day." I pressed the buzzer for the waiter and we exchanged twelve empty and somewhat spinachy oyster shells for two chicken Eugénie (under glass) and a bottle of red Puligny-Montrachet. I ordered baked Alaska for dessert, in advance. I thought of, but did not order, Mount Monadnock à la mode. I was having a good time on my birthday.

"How was the visit?"

"Dreamlike. I slept twelve hours a day. I had no responsibilities. Actually, you would have enjoyed the political electricity in the air, at the dinners and cock-tail parties—of which, by the way, everybody goes to at least three every night, if not five. Dress is 'smart casual,' open throat for men. You'd fit right in."

I resisted the impulse to tear off my necktie. "Sounds like my kind of town. I did three cocktail fund-raisers a night most of the time from June on. I'm always amazed when politicians say they can't stand fund-raising. I mean, if you can't sell yourself, what can you sell? It's almost my favorite part of cam-paigning, after the factory gates at five A.M. where you can see everybody's breath. What's the electricity, the handover to the Chinese?"

"The handover, indeed. In the white British trunks, we have"—and she waved her arm over her head like a referee. My goodness, I thought, I love the effect a glass of wine has on this woman. "In the white trunks we have the guardians of human rights everywhere, warning frantically that on July 1, 1997, the Communists threaten to repeal all the great statutory reforms, the basic rights of man safeguarded under British rule." She took another sip of the Puligny, warming to her topic. She was having a good time, too.

"In the black Chinese trunks, we have pesky practitioners of realpolitik, irritatingly pointing out that these basic rights of man were enacted in 1995, one hundred fifty-four years after the British took over and less than two years before the handover which had been agreed on a decade earlier. Furthermore, they have the gall to suggest that the Cantonese community in Hong Kong and South China is so disparate, so sprawling, that the political leadership of the nation, concerned about holding the country together, might pardonably distrust the 'human rights' offensive as the most antinationalistic principle imaginable. They've got to run a railroad, after all."

"I know the feeling. What do the white trunks say to that?"

She drained her glass and I refilled it. "They say, 'Bullshit, man. That's straight out of some self-justifying business school lecture.' I had to laugh, because of course it's exactly what my late husband used to preach and teach, and he was a business school professor, with plenty to justify. Anyway, the white trunks argue that's selective Confucianism, to say if anybody has any personal liberties the whole society is going to be transported straight back to the Warring States period."

"Sounds impressive. 'Selective Confucianism.' You don't mind if I use that in my next newsletter to our volunteer and donor base, do you?"

"I thought the election was over."

"The campaign is never over. Everything's computerized. The volunteers and donors can't escape."

She bowed her head and waved her arm again, this time magisterially. "Then be my guest, four-year campaign, sounds like you can't escape either."

I moved right along. Didn't want to tarry on *that* ground. "Anyhow, where do you come out?"

"I think I'm a black trunks man, I mean a black trunks lady."

"How so?"

She was instantly cold sober. I had seen this before. "Number one, the people in the street are already excited and happy about the transfer of power. They are hardly pining for another Western country to rush in and take care of them. Number two, anecdotal: I, or rather we, had two friends in the Hong Kong Civil Service who had gone to Oxford. P. C. Fang got a double first at Oxford—a starred first in Greats—and he couldn't get as good a job in the Civil Service as Simon Hollyhocks, who drank his way through the Gridiron and the Bullingdon Club and took a third. A low third." She glowered. "There's going to be some changes made come July; you heard it here first."

"You know, you understand everything I don't. Between the two of us, we've got the situation covered."

"Right, you can go do things, and I can sit by the fire and think Great Thoughts. Oh, I didn't mean to be short," she added, placing her napkin in my palm to fob me off. I realized my elbows were on the table. "It's just that you were doing such a crushing imitation of Lord Byron."

"Imitations are my long suit."

"I never said you weren't a good actor, just not a good liar."

"Ronald Reagan was a good actor. Maybe I'm in the right line of work."

"Only after he left the stage and screen. So maybe you are."

I heard two waiters in the corridor outside speaking German and Italian to each other. Emma heard also, and arched her eyebrows in approval. Nothing New World about this place. They knocked and entered with our dessert.

"*Rüdiger, wie läuft das Geschäft heute abend?*"

"*Ausgezeichnet, Herr Mullally, wir können uns vor Gästen gar nicht retten.*"

Rüdiger held the tray of baked Alaska at his waist. Emilio sprinkled it with Benedictine from a distance, then threw a match. The whole of Seward's Folly burst into blue flame. So did the entire front of Rüdiger's white tie, which had been liberally doused with liqueur by Emilio's casual arc. Rüdiger did not so much as flinch, held the plate steady, and Emilio batted out the errant flames with a huge linen napkin. Emma and I somberly studied the silverware.

When they had served and left us, I expected Emma to collapse in laughter. Instead she said, without a hint of gaiety, "I was in this room once at lunch with George LaSallières, do you know him?, the president of the Somerset Club, and one of the waiters came in and said there was a telephone call for him, and plugged a portable phone into the jack right there next to the buzzer, and proceeded to *turn around* and hold the phone *behind his back*, so we wouldn't think he was eavesdropping! Just so our Ganymede here—he bore his burden stoically!"

"It's a great place," I said stupidly.

"Another time, there was a rather late dinner of about twelve of us here, in the room down the hall, and after liqueurs, Ruthie excused herself and went to the ladies' but fell asleep in there. In the, uh, confusion, no one noticed her absence when we all drove back to Cambridge. She woke up at four A.M. and walked down the two flights of stairs in her cocktail dress and stiletto heels, right past the night watchman, who didn't bat an eye, just said 'Good evening, ma'am'—*not* 'Good morning'—and held the front door open for her. Didn't even ask if he could call her a taxi, figured she knew what she was doing."

"They treat you with respect here, don't they?"

"They treat you with respect."

The next week I signed a purchase and sale agreement for a brownstone town house on Commonwealth

Avenue in the Back Bay, just a block from the public garden (*not* "gardens," as I had learned from the book on Ruthie Truslow's coffee table—learned and remembered). Many of its features made me think of Emma: the woodwork, the old windows, even an *orangerie*. The broker said it was her easiest sale in thirty-four years, elapsed inspection time twelve minutes.

Emma in late December moved in enough of her things so we could stay together whenever we wanted, though she kept her place in Cambridge and spent a couple of nights a week there. She insisted on only one point: No secrets. No secrets, I said.

Within days of Emma's stocking a closet and bathroom, Jerry Traugott picked up word that Addie Stephens of the *Daily Mail* was working on a hatchet piece dealing with the town house. I was beside myself, figuring it had to do with Emma and living in sin. But Lanny and Jerry and I agreed we couldn't go directly to either Addie or to the brass of the paper, to try to wave them off: it would only excite them. We opted for having Jerry volunteer to Addie, in a vicious off-the-record girl-talk session, that I was sleeping with Emma and, in fact, living in sin with her, but that to Jerry's practiced eye, it looked like a long-term relationship— "equity investment, not debt," as Jerry put it. Turned out that Addie, unlike Ruthie's Auntie Vye, was much more interested in the chairs and other furniture than in what was on them. Her immediate response was "Oh, that's great! And this is happening in that million-dollar town house that he bought with—*what?* I thought he was from poverty."

We didn't go over Addie's head at the paper. Jerry relayed to her on background that I had saved my salary in New York and invested it successfully in the stock market, adding off-the-record: "You racist bitch. Just because *you* went to Exeter and Vassar! Nobody Irish is allowed to have any money? What would you print if he was *Italian?*"

Addie went with her story about the new DA's posh digs anyway, but she did put in our explanation at the end. And she never mentioned Emma or sin. Could have been a lot worse, I thought. Especially as I was, by definition, about to assume a much higher public profile.

chapter fourteen

My Funny Management Style

The second week in January, I got sworn in before six hundred of my closest friends by the governor himself. He was obviously bored silly with the proceedings. We had it at the IBEW union hall in Dorchester: already, I was sending a message for the reelect, just in case. I wore a Paul Stuart suit. Some of the union guys looked at my outfit like it was from *Star Trek.*

I didn't want ceremony that day, so we skipped the champagne party and went right back to the office on the sixth floor of the New Courthouse, which was the oldest courthouse in the city. There we had to mug for the cameras a little bit, and First Assistant District Attorney Francis X. O'Flaherty, who had been in the office forty-five years and was so old he wasn't buying green bananas anymore, slapped on the table a few indictments for me to sign while the TVs whirred.

I turned over my shoulder to O'Flaherty. "Isn't this a Rule Six-e violation?" I asked, referring to the federal law on grand jury secrecy. O'Flaherty just smiled a smile as vacant as some idiot French dauphin in the Middle Ages, stage-whispered "Five-d, state system now, sir!" and pushed the paper back in front of me, in full view of the reporters. This did not please me, partly because his body language screamed that he knew more than this lucky rookie. "I hope TV cameras can't read upside down," I muttered out of the side of my mouth to O'Flaherty. But I signed anyway. "This is easy!" I trumpeted. It was not hard to predict what would lead the nightly TV news, that goofy remark or an excerpt from my thirty-five-minute oration at the IBEW hall.

One campaign promise I was bound and determined to keep: In terms of hiring, I was going to run a merit office, not a political office. My sense was that nobody particularly believed I would do it—not most of the working press and clearly not the political and legal establishment. It was therefore with considerable relish that I used my first press conference, the day after my swearing in, to introduce Phil Vacco as the head of a newly created White Collar Crime Unit in the office.

Phil was accompanied by his delectable wife, Romy. She was of Central European extraction, looked like a Gypsy, and had quite recently spent two months stumping the length and breadth of Suffolk County on behalf of her husband and beating my brains in along the way. You couldn't prove it by her demeanor today. She took my politely proffered hand in both of hers, squeezed it rather than shook it, flashed her big black eyes at me and the cameras, and planted a slow kiss on my cheek. Not too close, but not an air kiss, either. She was beaming, and she was taking her time, which meant she wanted to be sure the stills got the shot. Lanny correctly predicted that both Boston dailies would have the photo of the kiss on page one the next day. "Republican Kisses Democrat? Man bites dog, they'll run it every time," he said. I wasn't sure I appreciated his analysis; for a few days, I snuffled and woofed at him whenever he had suggestions for me in private.

The public press conference, by way of contrast, saw nothing but our toughest game faces. The reporters were naturally ready with every anti-Mullally quote Vacco had used during the campaign. He shrugged them off—nice use of the net instead of the trident, I thought—and went on to explain that the *point* of his taking the job was that he and District Attorney Mullally shared a *vision* of the *proactive* job that had to be done to *protect* the *public*, et cetera. Lanny turned toward me, away from the cameras, and rolled his eyes in approval.

The veteran columnists were snide—"Mullally Gets an 'A' for Political Asininity" was the lead from the tough-guy crime-and-neighborhoods guru of the *Gazette*—but all the news reporters could do was to quote Phil Vacco. I didn't say a thing, and I've never looked better. It was a home run.

There was one little problem: If you're not going to hire people for political connections, you probably shouldn't fire them for political connections, either. So my initial plan was to keep on as many of Martin

Gross's assistant DAs as I could. This course was vehemently opposed by Lanny.

"They'll never be your people, Boss. You'll always have the downside, as long as they're here. Do your own thing, and take the upside. Important to take the upside. *You* know who you are, but *people* don't know who you are. Got to define yourself. By deed, not word. People are smart. They don't believe words, and they're right. They believe only actions."

It took precisely one week of 8:00 A.M. staff meetings to vindicate Lanny's view. It was depressing. The Old Guard and the new regime couldn't mix. At the first meeting, there was this old legal beagle who had been called "counselor to the district attorney" for the thirty-odd years since he lost a power struggle to be first assistant and heir apparent to some long-forgotten DA. He started giving me all kinds of free legal advice; actually, it wasn't free, because he was on my payroll, but I thought of it as free because I didn't ask for it.

First he advised me I had full power to wade into the middle of a huge, ugly street confrontation between prolife demonstrators and hecklers and the clinic access police, that is, Planned Parenthood. "Call 'em as you see 'em, Chief," he insisted, "but you've got the ticket."

I allowed as how I dimly recalled the attorney general—not the district attorney—had some equity powers under the civil rights laws, and could order people to stay so many feet away from a building and no farther, stand on one foot, put their hand on their head, and the like. He said that was true, but there was no law preventing me from rushing in. I told him I had already issued a press release during the campaign calling on the attorney general to intercede and bring order and calm to this volatile situation, pitting as it did, so unfortunately, the rights of well-meaning individuals of sincere conviction on both sides of this complex and very personal issue. Voting individuals, I noted. Like O'Flaherty, my counselor seemed puzzled by the obtuseness of the rookie.

He shrugged, made a little moue, and pressed on. His next piece of free legal advice was that I did *not* have the power to explore charges of criminal conspiracy against two utility executives who, according to the newspapers, had agreed to gouge the public by artificially inflating their rate base. Thus they would increase the monthly electric bill for every John Q. and Jane Q. in Suffolk County. This, my attorney advised me, was properly the purview of the attorney general under chapter 12 of the General Laws, given his broad injunctive jurisdiction to vindicate the public interest in rate cases.

"With all deference," I began—this was, for any trial lawyer, a well-understood euphemism for "screw you"— "I would rather have some *judge* tell me that." I glared around the room.

"Now I have a question for you," I said. "I'd like to file legislation to have special drug courts and special gun courts, to expedite those two classes of cases only, in Suffolk County only. What do you say?"

"Well, obviously, DA, if it's limited to only certain

classes of cases and certain geographic areas, that raises weighty legal issues, constitutional issues, even."

"Delbert, that's not the *answer*, that's the *question*, for Chrissake. I *know* the question, that's why I *asked* it! What's the *answer?*"

"Well, sir, it would be difficult to administer."

"Delbert, this is only a *proposal!* It still has to be enacted by the legislature, which it won't be because Chief Justice Sullivan hates it. And I'm not going to have to administer it in any case. Not my problem!"

"Good politics, maybe, but bad law, Chief."

"That's my point! The politics is all that's there! In the real world, given the opposition of the judges, this is not going to happen. So the legal questions fall away, they don't have to be answered. Let's keep our eye on the ball."

Maybe I had been a little too frank, because eyes rolled, and not in approval. I wasn't winning the Mr. Nice Guy Swimsuit Competition. The next day, I transferred Delbert to Winthrop and he quit.

The casualty of day three was Hugo DeFrance, the ancient and palsied press guy. This was one veteran who was literally grizzled: I thought he looked like Victor, an unforgettable corpse who was given by Cornell Medical School to a med student I was dating at the time, to experiment on. The first thing she had to do was saw his head in half horizontally, so she could look at his brain. It didn't change the fixed smile on Victor's face, nor did his six-day growth either disappear or turn silky. I always said to myself, "Now there's a stand-up guy; and if he can do it with half a head, how come there aren't more stand-up guys?" I carry that question with me still.

The grizzled veteran was all hot and bothered because there had been three items in the political gossip sections of the newspapers, one in the *Daily Mail* and two in the *Gazette*, about how I'd been treating lots of folks at Morton's and the Café Budapest and Olive's and having a wonderful time. I had seen the items: two of them carried a potentially sinister innuendo that I was spending money rather freely for a public servant. Hugo apparently had read right over that, though. His concern was the catty suggestion in all three pieces that I was putting on weight.

"Why is that bad?" I asked.

"It's undignified, Chief," explained the grizzled veteran. "If people think you're overweight and you eat too much, they'll laugh at you. Take it from me, as one who has been there and done that, once people start to laugh at you, you're finished in this business."

I appreciated this, of course, more than I could say, on my third day on the job. To have such heartfelt and personal advice delivered in front of fifty people, all of whom were watching me like a hawk, was particularly welcome.

"Hugo. Feed this story; do not starve it. Suggest lines for them, say, 'The DA loves to eat, and it shows,' or 'The DA has agreed to throw his not inconsiderable weight behind this project.' Better yet, let's give them a photo op! Tell the gossipers I will be sampling the delights of my district this very day by going to Filippo's, in the North End, and I intend to eat in the main dining room and have four full courses and they are more than welcome to come and photograph me. Plus, they will not have to come indoors, and thus use up their valuable time, because I will be seated at a window table."

"Chief, you are just going to get another story."

"Maybe a story, maybe not. Definitely a photo, with unkind caption."

"I'm afraid so, Chief."

"Hugo, nobody cares. Everybody's fat, or their spouse is. The press is seldom so innocently employed as when writing about the boss's waistline, as compared to the boss's outrageous power grabs and abuses of authority. Better peccadilloes than peculation, Hugo. Give 'em mock turtle soup, mock foibles, not the real thing!"

"Whatever you say, Chief." Another well-understood euphemism. Same meaning.

At the next morning's staff meeting I introduced Jerry Traugott as my deputy press secretary. Hugo came to see me later.

"Chief, I wouldn't criticize you for bringing in a woman, but she's not even a woman, she's a girl! She covered society stuff for the paper! You'll be laughed out of town!"

"She's a stone-cold killer, Hugo. She's not stupid, and what's more to the point, she's not emotional. She won't go for the bait. People trail phony bait in front of us all the time around here. I need somebody with a nose that can tell the real night crawlers. Now, good luck to you." This was also well understood. So Jerry got the top job after all, same day she reported for duty as only number two.

Another guy who seemed to be stuck in amber was the administrative officer, Honus Barnett. He had been a high school and college athlete, and he was still wiry, despite having a serious case of The Slows. I imagined he would brake for green lights, out of fear they might turn yellow.

Honus seemed to take an almost visceral pleasure in helping move my desk around the office; insisted on doing it himself. Not a delegator. "Yessir, we aim to please," he said once too often. Namely, once. His four favorite words, when a subject had been exhausted, were "While I've got you . . ."

Lanny and I decided that to be fair, we owed Honus an interview. "Honus," I began, "if there's one thing about the operation here you would change, what would it be?"

"If you please, sir, I wouldn't change a thing. If it ain't broke, don't fix it, as the man says."

Lanny excused himself from the room. He told me later he was so outraged by this answer he was afraid he might say something rude. So it fell to me to persuade Honus Barnett that he had put in a lifetime of work he could be proud of, and that he now wanted to enjoy his golden years on Carson Beach, with his bride. That's why they pay me the big bucks, I thought.

Fortunately, these guys all had good pensions.

*   *   *

I had gone to Marty Gross in early December, and said I knew he had an administrative first assistant, and I knew he had a legal guy, and I knew he had a press guy, but what I wanted to know was who was the real guy? "Who does your less desirable laundry, who makes it happen when skies are cloudy and gray?" I asked. Gross told me it was this retired sergeant Potts from the PD who handled the administrative-cum-political stuff and basically covered his flank and rear. Gross urged me to keep him. "When you're riding into Dodge City, you don't want to ride in alone," he advised me. "You want somebody covering your backside, and you may have to be riding back to back to keep an eye on all the Indians."

"Much obliged, Mr. District Attorney, I will keep this well in mind," I had said.

But the more I thought about it, the more I realized, Brendan Potts is not only not riding into Dodge City with me, he's tending the goddamn saloon before I even get there. So Potts went, too, to round out the first full week, and I brought in Lanny Green, twenty-four years of age with no law enforcement experience, as executive assistant district attorney. I was pretty sure the next campaign had already started, though as it turned out, I didn't know then what office it would be for.

When the routine settled down, the 8:00 A.M. staff meeting became my favorite part of the day. At thirty-three, I was the second oldest person in the room, after one of the few holdover ADAs, an appellate guy. Several of the younger lawyers I hired from the big firms were like colts: they had a lot of speed, but they could be stampeded and were liable to shoot off in unpredictable directions. By trial and error, I developed Mullally's First Law of Management: If anyone so much as raises their voice in discussing a topic, table it and bring it back for reconsideration the next day. After a while, people absorbed the message: Never let your irritation show. The tone became more professional.

With the exception of Phil Vacco, even my own hires seemed to lack the instinct for labor-saving accommodation that you necessarily pick up in a political campaign. They were constantly throwing elbows in the direction of the state attorney general's office, with whom we technically shared jurisdiction in most criminal cases. Henry Curcio had been reelected without opposition, and was widely disliked by both my staff and his own.

"He's a jerk, Boss," one of my red-hot blue chips said.

"That's not the question. The question is how can we maximize our own share of good cases over time, when we're basically locked into a four-year marital negotiation with this guy, and he can pull rank on us in any individual instance where he gets his back up. So the answer is, you give him one hundred twenty percent on the type of stuff he cares about, you try to make him look good, not bad, in the press, and he won't push us on the other stuff. Leave enough meat on the table for the other guy, so he'll want to do business with you again. In litigation, you figure out what the other guy doesn't want you to do and you do it; but in negotiation, you should make the other guy look good, not bad."

"DA, the police are upset with him."

"Don't ever tell me someone is 'upset'! That's nothing but a cover for failing to analyze the situation. When I was in private practice, I always loved it when people would threaten to sue a corporate client of mine, because it meant they had no business leverage left." I was feeling my oats.

"It would be helpful to look at things first from Curcio's point of view," I went on. "What does he want? How can we accommodate that to what we want?"

"Why should we start out by always trying to accommodate him? We'll just end up bidding against ourselves." The voice belonged to George Jerrell, a tall young blond fellow with enormous red ears who had apparently had a course in assertiveness training at the *Harvard Law Review*.

I rounded on him. "Don't confuse courtesy with weakness, George. There is absolutely no point getting dug in to a position early, in public. It limits your flexibility. You've then either got to crater the deal, or cave in—publicly. You should never force a client, much less yourself, to that choice. Both options have unacceptable costs."

"Then what's to prevent them from rolling us in every case?"

"We maintain hidden fortifications, we just don't dig them in public. If Babyface started really trying to throw his weight around, then there's plenty of time to call Reuben for lunch." Reuben was the head of Curcio's state police detail, and loathed him.

I summed up: "We've got to run a railroad? Curcio's got to run a railroad, too."

I could see my audience was unconvinced. I thought ruefully of Suffern's gibe when I left Brooklyn, calling me not a shark but an idiot. I wondered if I should tell them I sympathized with Elijah Low, who would saw a man in half if necessary for business reasons. But I noticed Lanny was nodding in agreement with my argument. And, besides, these other wizards hadn't just gotten themselves elected district attorney of Suffolk County after less than two years in Massachusetts. So I persisted in pushing the softer line. "There's plenty of crime for everybody," I said finally, and stood up, signaling the end of the discussion and indeed the meeting.

Three of the assistant DAs in the corner were so busy muttering mutinously to each other that they didn't notice I had stood up. I heard Curcio's name. Obviously, they were still hashing over the merits of what I had said. I didn't feel like having them drive my morning schedule—I had to get on to the next thing, three decision memos to pass on before a telephone call that had to begin in eight minutes—so I am afraid I kind of barked at them:

"Hey, FOLKS!" They turned around like deer in the headlights. Deer who had also been shot.

"Why don't we just do it my way? It will be easier for everybody."

They left, and the topic didn't come up again at a morning meeting.

In truth, I understood the frustrations of the young assistants. I remembered having felt much the same way myself, in the early years of my service under Tarzan Burroughs. Now I saw why Tarzan had always seemed to present his position with such force: it's a lot less tiring to lead than to follow. If all the ideas are your ideas, you don't have to worry about false trails and chicanes. Have you ever noticed, when the cabbie is driving, you hate the frequent stops and starts, but when you're driving, you don't mind them? Same thing.

In order to help newly arrived assistant DAs adapt to our culture, I had Lanny distribute little cards containing Mother Mullally's Helpful Hints. Some were Lanny's, most were mine:

1. Solve the problem yourself, that's why you're being paid more than four dollars an hour.
2. Never mind who gets the credit.
3. Play 'em like you got 'em.
4. Never let 'em see you sweat.
5. You never know where your next coalition is coming from.
6. You meet the same people going down as you did coming up.
7. If the boss asks you and you don't know, say so. Don't guess.

8. Take pleasure in doing little things well.

9. Always undersell; make the judge your advocate.

10. The district attorney makes only yes or no decisions, so make sure the question is "teed up." (See Hint #1, above.)

It was a little different from the clarion manifesto I had promised the *Daily Mail*, but I thought it was important to set down a few markers, to avoid wheel-spinning.

By the end of a few weeks in office, I had almost everybody in Boston's Old Boy legal community furious at me, but I also had my own team in place. I felt that if things went okay, I was poised to make good on my boast to the *Daily Mail* ed board, about attacking the power structure. And wouldn't you know, opportunity walked right in the door, whistling a happy tune, without even knocking.

chapter fifteen

Too Much Money

Once a guy realizes he can make a good living without doing an honest day's work, it's hard to persuade him to pick up the help wanted ads. So in law enforcement you run across the same crooks again and again. It's almost like keeping up with old friends. In my first five months as DA of Suffolk County, we had five heroin prosecutions against members of the Ghost Shadows gang, who had worked for my pals in the On Leong tong in Brooklyn and Queens.

You also get to meet new friends, like Stanley Wei, a/k/a the White Tiger, leader of the Ping On gang in Boston. Stanley hit the streets of Boston in March '97, when he was released from federal prison, but I had known him by reputation since my days in Brooklyn.

Stanley was a beautiful guy, a self-made man. He was an importer of gourmet frozen fish, stuffed with heroin, and beautiful Oriental rugs, saturated with heroin. Stanley had a lot of friends in other cities, particularly from the Wah Ching in San Francisco, the

Kung Lok in Toronto, and the On Leong in New York. He liked to travel with these friends, especially to Hong Kong, Mainland China, Burma, and Thailand.

Like many businessmen, Stanley Wei did not enjoy discussing his private business affairs. And so he refused to testify in front of the National Investigating Commission on Organized Crime, and spent thirty-six months in prison as a result. The feds extended the life of the grand jury, normally limited to eighteen months, to get him the second year and a half. And that second year and a half would cost him. Stanley should have bought business interruption insurance, but I guess John Hancock and the Pru don't write policies to cover situations like his.

Before going to prison in 1994, and during his first couple of years in the joint, Stanley had basically three productive lines of work in the Boston territory.

First was extortion of legitimate businesses, particularly those operated by Chinese born overseas. The importunings of Stanley's associates could produce a monthly "tribute" without even the necessity of a broken pane of plate glass, so well was the system understood. Every gig has its code.

The second line of business was illegal gambling in otherwise legitimate social clubs and restaurants.

Stanley's third line, and the most productive, was the laundering of money that had come from the narcotics trade, or which had entered the country from the Far East without having been declared on a Convertible Monetary Instrument Report.

One easy way to launder such funds was by having

the social clubs and restaurants declare revenues far greater than their actual receipts. Neither the state of Massachusetts nor the city of Boston nor Uncle Sam was ever heard to complain: they just collected their slice of the pie through income, meals, and sales taxes. In this way, the proprietors of a system that did not believe in reporting cash transactions were able to adhere to their preferred practices by simply paying a "tribute" to their new partners, namely, American government at all levels. It was an almost foolproof system.

The system had just two flaws. The first was qualitative: Stanley Wei didn't need foolproof, he needed IRS-proof. As soon as Stanley was in the can, nosy IRS net-worth examiners began hanging around the clubs and restaurants in Boston's Chinatown, asking to see the books. They even spoke Cantonese. Bad for business. Sort of like a uniformed cop hanging around a gay bar.

The other problem was quantitative: There was too much money coming into Boston from Hong Kong. The impending handover of the Crown Colony to the Chinese, scheduled for July 1, 1997, had the triad leaders panicked. Many of them had sided with Chiang Kai-shek against Mao decades earlier, or their fathers had, and they were not looking forward to the end of British rule. If every apartment in Chinatown had been a giant caravanserai with dancing girls, Stanley still couldn't have laundered all the specie his East Asian customers had for him. He needed institutional help. By the time Stanley hit the street, he knew he needed banks.

*   *   *

In the spring of 1997, I was still making the rounds of the other governmental agencies in town, and just after Easter I had invited Judy Boone, who ran the Federal Reserve Bank in Boston, to lunch in the men's bar at Locke-Ober's. She told me a curious thing: For the first time in history, her bank was taking in nearly three times as much cash as it was distributing to the commercial banks in the area. Some of this was legitimate investment from overseas, but Judy wondered about the magnitude of the disparity.

I didn't. I bet her a second lunch at Locke-Ober's it represented capital pouring out of Hong Kong, Burma, and Singapore, the fruits of narcotics distribution, alien smuggling, and the white slave trade. That night, I launched my theory on Emma, who said her British friends had told her tons of money were already fleeing Hong Kong the previous fall.

So Judy Boone and I decided it was time to go hunting together, in the Boston financial community. We were armed with subpoenas *duces tecum,* for documents, and subpoenas *ad testificandum,* for grand jury testimony. We were going hunting where the ducks are. That's how I like to do it.

The newly mobile Stanley Wei, an astute businessman, knew that if U.S. banks followed U.S. law, they would have to file Currency Transaction Reports and Convertible Monetary Instrument Reports, which held no appeal at all for Stanley's customers. He would never solve his cash volume problem.

His solution was simple. Having enjoyed a long track record of buying public officials on both sides of the Pacific Ocean, Stanley now set out to buy himself a network of private citizens. Citizens who worked in banks. Stanley was hungry for their help. Not surprisingly, Stanley got greedy. Stanley was a meat eater. So he went on a shopping spree.

The happy upshot was that in June, when Judy Boone and I slapped subpoenas on the back office operations of every bank in the Greater Boston area, we soon established that Stanley's people had been walking into highly esteemed financial institutions with suitcases of cash and walking out with bearer instruments. Understandable the customers wouldn't want to carry all that cash: a million dollars in twenties weighs a hundred pounds!

The propeller-heads who had been bribed tried their best not to leave any footprints, but the banks' internal controls got 'em every time. Nice paper trails: perfect for Phil Vacco's background in civil practice. Vacco killed them. Not one of those back office guys hung tough in the grand jury; they all spilled their guts right away. Not a long enough history of being bought. Like I say, there are surprisingly few stand-up guys these days.

They weren't terribly high-level bank officials, in any of the fifteen prosecutions we brought. But they were acting within the scope of their employment, with the intent of benefiting their employer: banks make money off money. And that was enough to hook the banks, criminally, said the First Circuit Court of

Appeals. Those cases wrote the book on corporate criminal liability, and Phil Vacco and I argued every one of them personally. One brand-name Republican, one brand-name Democrat: kind of hard for the defense to argue these were politically motivated prosecutions.

They say everybody's famous for fifteen minutes. They lie. When we had the arson cases in New York, I got a mention in the paper a few times. When we had the police corruption cases, I actually got my picture on the front page of the *New York Post* once, and in the B section of the *Times* twice. But when I convicted fifteen banks of criminal felonies in sixty-five days, from July to September of 1997, immediately following the handover in Hong Kong, my picture was on the front page of virtually every newspaper in the country. The good-government *Daily Mail* had to be pleased with their investment.

chapter sixteen

The Ferris Wheel

Those whom the gods would destroy, they first make famous, I guess, so you have to watch out. Maybe I should add that to Mother Mullally's Helpful Hints.

In the fall of '97, I was invited on every TV talk show in the country, not once, not twice, but as often as I'd come. National columnists, not high school kids, wanted to shadow me for a day. Publishers wanted to fly me to conference centers to talk to their advertisers. I will admit, it didn't take much getting used to. When you don't have to pay to fly first class, it gets harder to see the argument against it. I wasn't watching out, and I began accepting too many invitations from an uncharacteristically fawning media corps.

Lanny put a stop to it. "Wipe that smile off your face, Boss," he ordered. "The national press doesn't love you because of you. They could care less about any aspect of you. They want to use you to ruin other people, rich people, powerful people who work in buildings made out of Italian marble and thick glass that these hounds have never been able to penetrate before. They're sick to death of pressing their beagle noses up against the window of the Megabucks Bank Holding Company Building, always on the outside looking in.

"Moreover, not to get technical, of course, you don't have any *evidence* against these rich, powerful people. You convicted a bunch of artificial legal entities called corporations. You and Vacco did a good job, we can be proud of these cases, but we shouldn't set out to please the hounds. It's not your job, and you're not going to be able to satisfy them ultimately, anyway. They don't have to be consistent. Five'll get you seven they'll turn on you for grandstanding, unless you launch personal attacks that go beyond the four corners of the indictments, in which case Chief Judge Sacco will be pleased to punch your ticket for you. Either way, you lose."

I couldn't argue with Lanny's analysis, so after a week or so of preening on the national stage, I went into my prosecutorial crouch and got my game face back on. This whipped up the press into a further feeding frenzy—was I holding back on them?—but we hung tough.

The invitation from the U.S. Senate Finance Committee to testify about the great problems of our time, including possible federal money-laundering legislation, was another matter. Even Lanny had no problem with that one, and it was agreed I would appear at a 10:00 A.M. hearing on November 6. What a difference a year makes.

The invitation was particularly tangy because the

second-ranking Republican on the panel was the not-so-distinguished junior senator from Massachusetts, Harold Dellenbach. Dellenbach had been in for three terms and would be up again in '98. He was a stick-in-the-mud Republican, a former insurance executive, cagey and smarmy but no rocket scientist. Though short and fat, he had become a successful lecher in Washington. While the press had given him a pass on this weakness, a few reporters did suggest that Dellenbach seemed to have become lazy in office. He had come under fire for a spotty attendance record, particularly at subcommittee meetings of the Finance Committee. His name and mine had already been linked in more than one *Gazette* and *Daily Mail* col-umn—and I don't mean romantically. MULLALLY COULD TAKE OUT DELLENBACH was the not-too-subtle head on a Sunday op-ed piece by Dan Watkins in the *Daily Mail.*

Whether because of this, or because of a late evening, Senator Dellenbach seemed more than a little out of sorts when my turn came and I took my seat at the witness table in the gilt-edged Senate Finance Committee hearing room. In my ten-minute opening presentation, I summarized the facts of our fifteen cases and recommended two legislative measures to tighten up currency-reporting requirements. Dellen-bach fidgeted and fussed with his papers the entire time.

The committee chairman was the ever-urbane Stanley Greaves of Delaware. Cordial but a tad cool in view of my party registration, he opened the question-ing by noting that nowhere else in the country had a bank been convicted of criminal money laundering, yet here were fifteen count-'em fifteen banks in one metropolitan area, convicted in a little over two months. Was there something in the water in Boston? he asked. He was sure these transactions were highly unusual, he said.

Now Dellenbach, in a violation of protocol he was to regret, interrupted and contradicted his own chairman. "I beg to differ!" he burst in. "Those of us who are familiar with the financial services industry in this country, as I am, know full well the enormous pressures that exist on individual bank branches to attract and retain deposits of funds. No one has suggested that the management of any of these fine institutions"— which of course had been fattening his campaign coffers with contributions for two decades—"has been guilty of any offense or even of any misjudgment. The misconduct, if any, occurred at a very low level. Given the nature of the competition in this industry, I am certain it happens in every geographic area with equal frequency. The financial institutions of Boston, I dare to say, have a reputation, and a deserved one at that, second to none in the country."

Dellenbach was playing to his financial base. That's a smart thing to do if you're at a private meeting, or a fund-raiser. It's not so smart if you're on C-Span, live and nationwide, because what appeals to your financial backers is quite likely to sound unappealing to the voting public at large, as well as to the media.

Chairman Greaves, obviously irritated but smiling

broadly, turned and fed me a softball. "What do you say, Mr. Mullally?"

"All I would venture, Mr. Chairman, is that if these activities are occurring all over the country, as the distinguished senator from my home state suggests, they are nonetheless illegal activities, and should be prosecuted and stopped wherever they occur. They do, after all, cover up and facilitate other criminal activities such as narcotics trafficking, alien smuggling, and the white slave trade."

Boom.

The chairman laughed softly and said, "Yes, Mr. District Attorney, I think we can all agree on that." He tactfully avoided looking at Dellenbach, but he was the only person in the room to display that tact. Dellenbach turned a deeper red than usual, rose and disappeared into the holding room behind the dais. There was such a buzz from the audience and the press that the chairman gaveled a recess.

The 1998 campaign for the U.S. Senate seat had begun. And it had begun with a defining moment.

I knew enough not to stick around and give interviews, which could only complicate or confuse what looked like a delightfully straightforward story line. So I slipped out as the press was descending on the Members, hustled to National and caught the one o'clock US Air. I got back to the office in Boston around three-thirty.

As soon as I settled behind my desk, I asked to see Lanny. I thought I knew, but I wanted reality check on the enormity of the event in Washington. I was told

Lanny was in the conference room, and I could see him there. This struck me as a little odd, but I was in a good mood, so I said I could see Jerry Traugott instead. I was told she was in the conference room, too. That struck me as really quite odd, so I padded down the hall and pushed open the big oak door to cries of "Shenatoor!" and "Dishtrick of Clum-bya, hay we come, rye back whey we shdarded fwum!" The table was littered with cigarette butts and empties, and they were both knee-walking drunk. I didn't begrudge it to them, under the circumstances, and none of the three of us has ever mentioned this episode since. All I said was "I believe I'll leave you two lovebirds alone." There was no interest along that line, though, just delirious joy over a perfect inning in the Game.

The evening TV captured Dellenbach's blunder in living and loving color. All three Boston networks, plus Fox and 56, had pundits speculating about my entering the '98 race. The tabloid *Gazette*, normally sympathetic to Republican points of view, filled its Friday front page with the photograph of Dellenbach unmistakably choking with rage, under the splash headline GOTCHA!

Heads like that don't come around too often in my line of work.

Just when you think that diet of fat pitches is going to go on forever, the Big Guy deals you a fastball right at eye level. This one came in the third week of November. Everything was great at the office, everything was even better on Commonwealth Avenue, when the receptionist interrupted a Thursday senior staff meeting to ask if Detective Lieutenant Solano from New York could join us. I said of course.

"Very sorry, DA. It's about Elijah Low"—he looked around the room at the others—"who, you know, used to be married to Emma." Here he lowered his eyes. Emma and I were, after all, living in sin. But he soldiered on. I affixed a pleasant and interested smile to my face, where it froze.

"I thought I should come up to let you know this in person, DA. The Hong Kong police, the new guys, not the Royals, have reopened the case. So far just photos and documents, no exhuming, but they're now saying it was murder, at least the woman was strangled before the car crash, and they think they see a small-bore pistol entry in the male victim that was missed earlier, probably twenty-two caliber."

I received this news in silence. All I could manage was "Do they know who might have done it?"

"They have a suspect in custody, a Vietnamese. Apparently he was overheard discussing it."

Again I couldn't think of anything to say except "Thank you, Lieutenant."

"I'm sorry, DA," said Rudy, and left. It took a considerable exercise of will on my part to resume and conclude the staff meeting.

I went over to Emma's law office to report the news. She did not take it well, nor would I have expected her to.

"How the hell does Rudy know all this?" she cried with some exasperation.

"He's close to the scene in Hong Kong, has worked

a lot of Asian, ah, cases," I said. "I'll see if I can't get a channel other than Rudy."

"Yes, do that. Please." She turned away, and I left. I didn't want to lock eyes with her.

Rudy called the office late that day and came back to see me alone in my office the next morning, as I had expected he might. He looked a little green around the gills and his cigarette was trembling.

"They want to talk to me, Boss."

"Who does?"

"The Hong Kong police. The new guys, the ChiComs, not the Royal HKs, whom we knew and loved."

"I see," I said. I hesitated a little. "The suspect in custody, is it Olie Wing?"

"Yes," said Rudy. Neither of us said anything for a while. Rudy puffed a lot on his gasper.

"Rudy, did you talk to Olie about this?"

"What do you mean, did I talk to him? You did everything but buy me the plane ticket over there! Besides, Olie owed us big-time, as you may recall."

"Oh, bullshit, Rudy. You and I never discussed any of this. I'm absolutely certain of that."

"Whatever you say, Boss. But I'm not deaf, dumb, and blind, you know. And we sure as hell did more than discuss the other thing, back when." More silence. I felt dizzy. My world was crashing again.

Rudy said, "Sorry, Terry. But I don't feel good. I think I'm going to get some fresh air in my lungs in New Hampshire this weekend and think this all through. Think everything through, you know."

He smiled and put his hand on my shoulder. It took everything I had not to knock it away.

"I think Olie will be okay. He should know—hell, he does know—how to keep his mouth shut. I'm just worried, is all."

"Sure, nobody likes things being, uh, unpredictable." I stammered. "Di-did you say anything to Olie about, uh, well, about me?"

"Never did, never have. Not then, not now. Doesn't know you exist."

I relaxed a little, but not much. I also decided I had asked Rudy quite enough questions. That last exchange would not sound great if played back on a tape recorder. And you never know.

"I just gotta go clear my head," Rudy repeated.

"Sure, Rudy," I said. "I understand. Good luck."

I jumped at the sound of the door clicking shut behind him. I was thinking the Ferris wheel had taken me from the top of the mountain to the bottom.

The next day was my birthday, which means it was the day my mother died. Rudy wasn't the only one with a lot to think about.

chapter seventeen

Trouble in the Woods

I felt unsteady the rest of the day Friday, and left the office early. But in public life, the animals must be fed and the show must go on, so that night, Emma and I and Lanny took in a meal for the ages with Dan Watkins of the *Daily Mail* and Lorenzo Kettaneh of the *Gazette*, at Morton's in Copley Square. Lots of oysters, surf and turf Béarnaise, artichokes and salsifies hollandaise, noble South African whites, noble Chilean and Australian reds, soufflés, stingers, champagne— quite a production.

"Terry, this is *sinful*," Watkins opined cheerily, picking his teeth.

Kettaneh concurred. "All those lobsters, this is worse than *Vietnam*, for Chrissakes."

"I know," I said with resignation. "You're right. But we've got to take our pleasures where we find them."

This insight silenced the members of the Fourth Estate, who proposed several witty toasts to pleasure and finally looked on without moving a muscle as I picked up the check.

It had started to snow heavily as Emma and I walked home. She, in fact, had some difficulty negotiating the sidewalk. The weather reports were calling for a foot or more, all over New England.

Emma crashed onto her bed back at the town house. I covered her with two quilts, gave her a kiss on the forehead—nobody at home there, for sure—and turned off the light. She was out for the long count.

I went down to the basement closet where I keep all my outdoor stuff. I got out a loden coat and my heavy equipment bag. I put on my sixteen-inch boots and went outside to check on the beautiful storm. The outdoors is my cathedral, remember, and not just in fair weather. I'm like Ishmael: there's a lot of November in my soul.

Early the next morning, I called Lanny at the apartment in Bay Village to ask him to come over to Comm. Ave. at eight, which he did, although he was obviously wrestling with a head. I made a point of telling him I felt quite chipper, having stuck to two glasses of delicious South African white at Morton's. As Lanny and I went over the press hits for the coming week, Emma was audibly still out of it in the bedroom. She staggered in around ten complaining of the worst headache she had had in years. I recommended two Bayer, but Lanny proposed hair of the dog: "Don't nurse a hangover, doctor it!" he urged persuasively.

Lanny lasted two and a half hours before leaving

to follow his own advice. Emma, looking mussed and therefore particularly ravishing, had settled down to some breakfast cereal on a stool in the kitchen.

"Come out here for a minute," I called winningly from the sofa.

"Don't you play coy with me, Terry Mullally, I know you. And I don't want my raisin bran to get soggy."

I stepped over to the kitchen doorway and made a mock scale of justice in front of me with my palms. "Terry Mullally," I nodded to my right, "meet raisin bran," nodding to my left. "Plunk!" I exploded, as my left hand sank heavily and my right rose helplessly. Emma was mildly amused, but not so much so that I got my way.

"It's my birthday!" I pleaded. No sale.

We picked up Lanny and his Nigerian friend Oliver at around noon. Lanny was deep in a copy of *Homo Ludens*, by Johan Huizinga. I asked him what it was about. Emma rolled her eyes.

"It's my favorite book. You should love it. It's all chess, Boss. Chess and volleyball."

"What is?"

"Everything!" cried Lanny and Emma with one voice.

I was glad for the cover of the movies. We took in a double feature at the Nickelodeon: *Buckaroo Banzai* and *Repo Man*, two of my favorites. I was only sorry we couldn't stay for *Hudson Hawk*, a superb Bruce Willis sci-fi. But we had birthday dinner plans, important plans: Sissy and Brad Parmelee of the *Daily Mail*.

We never made it to dinner. At seven, just as I was primping in front of the mirror, the police dispatcher beeped me. "Roz," I said, "you know I hate being called at home, particularly on a Saturday."

"DA, it's the commissioner," she said. She seemed stressed. I waited. In about thirty seconds, which is a long time for this genre of communication, he came on the line. "Hello!" he barked. He all but incorporated name, rank, and serial number into that one word. He and I just barely got along.

"Georgie, boy, how ya doin'?" I opened brightly. I really didn't care for this fellow. I was pumping up my own energy level so as not to get caught hating him.

"Not too good, DA." I could tell it was a mistake having addressed him by his first name. "There's been an accident, a bad accident."

My voice dropped an octave. "Oh, shit," I said. "Many hurt?"

"No, sir. It's Rudy Solano."

"Automobile?"

"No, sir. He apparently went up deer hunting yesterday to that place he has in New Hampshire, in Cheshire County. Somebody from the job called in when he didn't make it to Lowell this after, and the New Hampshire staties went and found his car there, and I'm sorry to say they also found him, three-quarters buried in the snow, with a bullet clean through his chest. Went right by his heart. He's gone."

"Oh, Jesus, Jesus. Was it his gun?"

"Don't know. His gun has been fired once, four

shells still in the magazine. Entry and exit wounds consistent with his gun."

"Where was his gun?"

"It was where it would be, if, you know . . . "

"Commissioner, I'm getting up there right now, and I don't want to be at the wheel. Please have Sergeant Gatto over here pronto, four-wheel drive. And let me tell you this: Rudy Solano would never, ever, put a bullet in himself. He enjoys life! Enjoyed life. I'm gonna get up there and make sure they don't screw this up. Who's in charge of the investigation?"

"Chief is Charlie Parenteau, out of Jaffrey."

"I know Parenteau. He's a good man. Straight shooter. Is Gatto coming?"

"Relax, he'll be there in one minute, he's just coming from Berkeley Street." There was a pause. "DA, you should know, Chester Parrish is on the scene, too."

"Oh, *shit*, George. Parrish is running for pope. He'll kick this thing so far into the center field alley they'll never find it in the outfield grass."

"DA, one other thing I should tell you?"

"Yeah. Go ahead."

"Senator Dellenbach's office has called, asking for information about what happened."

"Oh, I see. Before you called *me*?"

"I'm just telling you what happened. Sir."

"Okay, thank you. Good-bye, Commissioner."

"So long, Terrence."

Terrence. We were even.

Gatto and I were on the scene near Jaffrey in an hour and forty minutes, even with the snow. Rudy's

Tahoe, except for the yellow tape around it, looked just like any of the other police vehicles that had come to the scene—which I guess it was. Chester Parrish was in my face before my foot was off the running board: "Greetings, Honorable District Attorney, and welcome to New Hampshire! I see you forgot your boots!"

This just thrilled me. I waved him off disgustedly. Parrish was a wholly owned subsidiary of Harold Dellenbach, who hailed from Gardner, Massachusetts, right down the road. And Parrish was an ambitious, publicity-seeking county attorney. As well as a total moron.

"Shut up, Chester. Where's Parenteau?"

"He's over there, but you don't have to be a complete jerk about this, just because—"

"I said *shut up!*" I made my way past the media horde, who were being restrained by barriers from moving any farther into the woods. Pierre Lamarque, from Parenteau's office, led me three hundred yards or so into the woods to the scene. My shoes were completely submerged in the snow. It looked like well over a foot had fallen that day.

We came up behind Parenteau as he was still looking down at the body. There was a lot of red.

"Bad business, Charlie," I said.

Parenteau turned around and seemed startled to see me. "Boss, it's you!" he said. He and I had gotten to know each other at DAs' meetings and some Democratic political affairs. I considered him a law enforcement pro.

"Not his gun?" I inquired.

"We're still looking for the bullet. Entry and exit consistent with his three-oh-eight. Faint powder burns, but he's been in the snow awhile. Medical examiner did field tests, time of death midnight to four A.M. this morning. That's a problem for a second-hunter theory, if it holds up."

"Not your most popular deer-hunting hours," I acknowledged.

"Right, Boss. No moon or stars last night, either, just snow. ME's tentative read is suicide. I'm thinking, something was eating Rudy, something we don't know about, and he maybe wanted to go out where he's comfortable. He loved it around here."

"I know he did, Charlie. But I don't think this was Rudy, on purpose. You say nobody can get shot in the dark? You'd be amazed what goddamn hunters can do, particularly guys from the city. Guy in Western Mass. killed a perfect stranger last November with a shotgun, shot him point-blank, thought he was a *turkey*, 'cause the guy had white hair and the shooter had read that turkeys have white heads. Never seen one. City slicker takes a brush shot, or can't see 'cause it's too dark or he's too drunk, he'll kill you as soon at five yards as at five hundred."

"Ain't that the truth," said Parenteau.

"And I see another problem," I said.

"What's that?"

"What the hell is Rudy Solano doing in the middle of a bunch of alders six inches apart? He wants to find a partridge, chowing down on a nice alder leaf, or an apple, maybe, he should be in terrain like this. But deer?

Never. You wouldn't find a deer in these alders. Not enough cover, plus, they can't run. And what's he doing with those big Michigans?" I pointed at one of Rudy's snowshoes, the only one still visible. "Look at the tail on them. You wouldn't go into alders with them on. You'd want Vermont Trappers, no tail. Something doesn't fit. Any possibility the body has been moved?"

"We asked ourselves the same question, Boss, but completely impossible to tell. Foot and a half, two feet, all today and yesterday. The blood goes pretty deep here, but not all the way to the ground."

I processed this information. Then I called over Parrish. "Listen, Chester," I said. "I know this is not my state and I know this is your case. And I'm glad you have Charlie Parenteau on it with you. But before you even get to that bullet, I'm telling you there is no way Rudy did this. He's just not that kind of guy. Besides, he had no reason to. Everything has been going great for him, he's never been busier at the PD in New York. Forget politics this once. I respectfully request you keep me posted up to the minute on what you're getting. Because there is no way Rudy took his own life." And I broke down, I guess, a little, because Parenteau came over and clapped me on the shoulder and said, "Sure, DA. We got it under control. And we'll keep you in the loop. Now you go get some rest."

I cried my eyes out in the truck on the way back to Boston, thinking about Rudy and me, about Rudy and my father, about my father and me. Gatto was embarrassed. He told Roz, the dispatcher, that he'd never seen a man cry like that, even on the witness stand.

chapter eighteen

Taking It and Dishing It Out

Because Chester Parrish is such a moron, he didn't want responsibility for anything attaching to him, so he requested the Cheshire County coroner to conduct an inquest regarding the cause of Rudy's death. The coroner empaneled a jury in early December 1997, and took testimony from a number of Rudy's colleagues, as well as from the medical examiner who had conducted the forensic tests.

At the time, I was actively considering a Senate bid against Harold Dellenbach in 1998, and Lanny and Jerry were desperate to keep me a million miles away from the bad publicity surrounding any suicide or unexplained death. But I insisted on testifying at the inquest. I told Lanny I knew the politics were bad, but that it was a necessary catharsis.

I was the only witness who publicly questioned the suicide theory. I testified that I had known Detective Lieutenant Solano since he was a sergeant on the NYPD, that I knew him to be a person of fine character and considerable discipline, and that I thought all investigative avenues needed to be explored before the jury was permitted even to consider a verdict of suicide, which I considered most unlikely, based on my knowledge of the decedent.

On cross-examination, I was asked if Lieutenant Solano had had any unsavory associates, and replied, "None other than those he prosecuted." This got a laugh in the room, so I looked around for the first time, and noticed to my displeasure a flack from Dellenbach's office sitting in the front row taking notes.

I went into my theory that there was something odd about Rudy being in thick alders if he was deer hunting on snowshoes, but the coroner cut me short, saying he was interested only in facts and not in theories. He got me to acknowledge that Rudy was a seasoned hunter, and that an accidental discharge of his rifle was virtually out of the question.

Finally, after I had gone on at some length about Rudy's zest for life, I did have to admit that he had seemed a little out of sorts shortly before his fatal weekend trip. This only confirmed what a number of his colleagues had already testified to. As soon as the coroner got that admission from me, he rested and submitted the case.

The coroner's jury was out twelve minutes and came back with a verdict of suicide. The consensus of the press, according to Jerry and Lanny, was that I had just been trying to save the reputation of a friend, and that I had not done a very impressive job of it, especially for a guy who had tried so many jury cases. I told them I was glad I had testified anyway.

Life at the New Courthouse went on, in any event, as District Attorney Terrence Mullally, Jr., began his second year in office. We got a nice break in a public corruption case, when a Minnesota businessman who had been shaken down on a City of Boston contract marched disgustedly into my office, reported the whole thing, and agreed to wear a wire for us. The result was the high-profile guilty plea of a department head and a city councillor. They didn't have much choice, we had mousetrapped them beautifully.

While the filing deadline wasn't until May, the press was increasingly interested in me taking on Harold Dellenbach. The political reality was that if I didn't take the plunge, there was no one else in either party who would help them sell newspapers through the 1998 election cycle.

I had pretty good statewide name recognition, because of the cases involving the banks, but everybody recognized it would be uphill against Dellenbach. He had been in for eighteen years and had been state treasurer for eight years before that, so he not only had a seasoned statewide organization, he had a truckload of money. The initial polling by WBOS-TV in late January of '98 had it Dellenbach 58, good guys 21. By late February, it was Dellenbach 54, good guys 27.

Lanny and I were not dismayed with the political situation. For one thing, there were obvious parallels with the earlier race against Martin Gross, and Lanny and Jerry saw to it that these parallels were painstakingly explored by two of the dumber weekly columnists, one for each major daily. Actually, they were not dumb, it was just that they were willing to take dictation. Lanny and I always stood up for them when our people privately criticized them for being feckless: "Because these guys get paid without working, we're supposed to think they're *stupid?*" It was like Emma's really stupid dogs, so-called.

For another thing, Dellenbach had not had a tough race since his first reelect, and twelve years is a long time to let the head muscles atrophy, let alone the leg muscles. Witness his bonehead play at the Finance Committee hearing. He knew Washington, for sure, but we were not sure he still knew Massachusetts. If we could make the campaign a gigantic eight-month St. Patrick's Day roast, we thought we might trip him up.

As in 1996, the Feast of the Saint was the unofficial kickoff for the race. We got off to a fast start in the Merrimack Valley.

The Lowell breakfast was at the Sheraton, née the Hilton. No heavy lifting required, but Dellenbach's rusty machine let him make several errors.

Number one, he arrived at 8:45 A.M. instead of 7:00 A.M. If 7:00 A.M. had been good enough for the aristocracy of Lowell—to coin a phrase—for the last eleven years, it should have been good enough for Dellenbach.

Number two, he gave a policy speech about the issues in the Senate race. Nobody truly wants to hear a politician discuss issues, either at seven in the morning anywhere or in Lowell ever. "Show me a candidate who talks issues within three weeks of the Feast, and I'll show you a loser," I told a staff meeting.

Number three, the senator's remarks could have been delivered anywhere. He did not delve into the latest scandal on the City Council, or roast the district's notoriously absentee congressman, or talk about the fabled sense of humor of the mayor (he had none), or make snide references to the diseases that could be picked up at Kenny's Place or The Rusty Nail, two local bars eternally locked in mortal combat for the bottom of the barrel. He aimed no shafts at the powerful and conservative local newspaper, the *Moon*, whose publishers had run the town for twenty-five years and who did not at all mind mixing it up at this particular breakfast. He didn't comment on the state of labor relations in the city. He did not even question how the city manager got his job.

My remarks, by way of contrast, did all these things and nothing more. No issues. And Jerry had me there at 6:50 A.M., so I got to do two live and friendly radio feeds outside before the doors of the dining room even opened. (Radio talk show hosts believe that everything that is, is wrong. Hence they are a gift from heaven to political challengers, to make up in part for a lot of other indignities which challengers must undergo.)

The coverage in the *Moon* was savage. They painted a vivid word picture of a stumbling, sweating, out-of-touch troglodyte who was doubtless late because he had gotten lost attempting to find the city. They noted three mispronunciations: one mayor and two city councillors. Not a good average.

If those were mistakes of the beta degree, at Hibernian Hall in Lawrence, Dellenbach made alpha errors. Following the breakfast fiasco, his staff obviously scrambled to cobble together some caustic material regarding the city fathers in Lawrence, and particularly the Connors family, which had been prominent in the city's councils for over two generations. Easy target, you'd think, because as usual, Old Man Connors was the official emcee for the luncheon.

Problem was, Old Man Connors was dying of cancer, and everybody in the city knew it, except for, apparently, the Dellenbach people. If the acoustics weren't so bad in Hibernian Hall, you could have heard a pin drop as Dellenbach, roaring at his own satirical wit, lit into the dying man.

After his funny intro, Dellenbach began plowing through a prepared speech. Nice move. Any Lawrence native over the age of six could have told him one does not *speak* at Hibernian Hall on the Feast Day of the Saint. One *sings*. There are green jackets and ties and green dresses and green carnations everywhere, but, above all, there is green beer in abundance, and no one either wants to or can possibly hear a normal voice.

Johnny Connors, the great-nephew of Old Man Connors and a strong Republican, mercifully interrupted Dellenbach's canned text and asked if he would like to sing a song for the crowd. Said Hughie and Gootch would accompany him on the accordion and piano. Dellenbach tried to shrug it off with a wave, but his failure to perform on those boards did not go unnoticed. The local paper, the *Hawk*, was somewhat gentler than their cross-Valley competitor in Lowell, but a lot of damage had been done.

Given this beginning, some of our field people were disheartened when the *Daily Mail* ran a page-one story the next week on a poll showing Dellenbach ahead 49 percent to 26 percent in a trial heat, and declaring him to be "untouchable in his race for reelection to a fourth term for which there is ample precedent in this State."

It didn't slow Lanny or me down at all: number one, count the undecideds against the incumbent, and number two, reporters and columnists would remember that word "untouchable." While stropping their razors.

We announced officially on March 24, in Springfield, New Bedford, Worcester, Lowell, and Boston. It felt right. We had plenty of time. I am a patient guy. I'll sit in the back of a courtroom or the back of a tree all day.

There were a couple of intangibles working for us. The media people, for example, could see that I was as comfortable with them as Dellenbach was uncomfortable. Lanny regularly scheduled one-on-one off-the-record chats for me with seasoned reporters, just to permit a mutual taking of the pulse. Dellenbach's people would sooner have locked him in his office with a leper. They understood they would pay a price for this, but they knew their man and they were right. Sometimes you just have to grin and take the downside.

In one such session, I treated Lorenzo Kettaneh to my theory that prosecutors and press generally get along well because we both attack the power structure. He shook his head.

"Reason we get along, DA, has nothing to do with tilting at windmills. It's you guys understand we're in the same business, Dellenbach's people don't."

"Oh? What's that?"

"The entertainment business. Welcome to the stage."

I didn't tell him that no less an authority than Emma Gallaudette agreed with him.

Our pollster, Snoopy Smullins, was quite a piece of work. At one meeting, our research director—I now had to have one, since I didn't know the Senate issues yet—was arguing that statistics showed community policing had been successful in reducing crime and we should back off our criticism of Dellenbach for sponsoring the program.

"Listen, kid," Snoopy moaned. "The only statistics I care about are the overnight tracks, and we've moved up eight points on this guy in the last five days by hammering his brains in on the community policing issue. So don't give me any garbage about substance or reality."

Snoopy was a real presence, a confirmed logorrheic. He had one gear: overdrive. I found him so entertaining that I wanted to follow all his recommendations, but I learned I had to apply Lanny as a kind of filter on Snoopy—or was it a blotter?—to save me from myself.

Snoopy wanted to hire Fred Wertz as a consultant, said he was brilliant. Lanny rose up like a mother lion. Who's Fred Wertz, I asked innocently.

"Fred Wertz is the wet boy of East Coast Democratic politics," Lanny spat out. "He does wet work. Hire him, I'll guarantee you he'll have guys painting 'Gardner Sanitation Department' on the side of a truck, be picking up Mr. and Mrs. Dellenbach's garbage every single day."

Sure enough, in the late summer, Wertz got nailed going through the garbage of the opponent of one of his clients. We were well out of that one.

Snoopy also wanted to do "push polling," to stir up the pot a little. I said, Whazzat? Lanny said, "Oh, nothing, really. Instead of telephoning four hundred people and asking them forty-eight questions about the race, you telephone twenty thousand people and ask them one question, a hypothetical: 'Would it make any difference to your vote if you learned that Senator Harold Dellenbach had just been caught in bed with a chicken?' or some such. The point is the question, not the answer. The hope is with that size sample, people will talk and the premise of the question will become a rumor and next thing you know it'll be getting into the water table, i.e., the weekend political chitchat columns."

I wheeled on Smullins. "Snoopy, is this true?" I asked in mock alarm.

Snoopy hung his head, like his namesake.

"So," I said, turning to Lanny, "your point is it's unethical?"

"Hell, no, Boss. My point is, if you get caught, which you're likely to with that many interviews, the *Daily Mail* will kill us. Once they ask if we did this poll, we can't deny it. Direct lie to the press is the one big no-no, game misconduct."

Once again, Lanny was prescient. One of the candidates for Congress in the Sixth, a woman, got forced out before the primary because she had to admit doing push polling, implying one of her two opponents wanted to legalize prostitution. No basis in fact. The Lynn and Salem papers savaged her daily and nightly, and drove her right out of the race. She was a client of Fred Wertz, too.

Lanny, in fact, made all kinds of kick saves in the goal mouth for us. In May, virtually everybody on the Democratic ballot got caught up in a minor fund-raising scandal because of a Korean guy who had bundled contributions and delivered them to a host of unwary candidates, including us. When the story broke, everyone was in denial—everyone, that is, except us. On Lanny's advice, we returned at once every contribution from anyone with an Asian surname, Korean or not, related or not, even contributions from longtime friends and supporters. And we said we were sorry, even though we weren't. If you don't really mean it, it's okay to apologize, apparently.

"Same news trough, Boss," Lanny said. "Doesn't matter that you're innocent. No such thing with the press. They are running with this for the next three weeks, no matter what anybody says, because the public thinks it's tangy. You can be in the day-two story and the next twenty stories, or you can be out of them. Up to you, us. The only way to be out of them is to cut and cut cleanly right now, same news trough. My view."

"So I should do the wrong thing, just because if I don't, the press will tattoo us?"

"*Very* good! Boss, we will make a politician out of you yet, or at least a *candidate*."

Same News Trough—never be in a day-two story unless you want to be—was one of Lanny's Little Laws, which everyone on the campaign had internalized by the end of the race. Two others were: We're on the Same Side as the Press (the Abe Fortas gambit), and Never Worry About Leaks (because they let off steam from within the organization).

Harold Dellenbach could have done a lot worse than to sign up for a tutorial with Lanny, but somehow I wasn't worried about that happening.

In June, Lanny sent me to talk to a group of advocates for increased spending on human services.

"Remember, Boss: 'Message: I care.'"

"But, for Chrissakes, Lanny, I don't care, at least not the way this crowd does. I'm not a busybody. I want people to be left alone. Remember, if the Edsel was a government program, it would still be around and it would be forty feet long."

"Can't say that, Boss."

"Well, what about emphasizing the federal government shouldn't do all this stuff directly, it's not free money, that sort of thing?"

"Can't say that either. Go at Dellenbach's throat on this."

"But this is one area where his record doesn't appall me. I would have voted basically the same way."

"Doesn't matter what you think. You're only one vote, fortunately. Nobody will believe it. He's a Republican, you're a Democrat. Case closed. It'll take him a million bucks of thirty-second spots to dig out from under this."

"Can't I say *anything* that's true?"

"Sorry, Boss. You gotta sneak around to his left on the 'I care' stuff, for Newton and Brookline, and to his right on the welfare stuff, for Everett and Malden and Waltham and the West. We're beyond just Suffolk County now."

"In other words, the opposite of the truth, on both issues."

"You said that, not me."

"I used to be such a nice boy before I met you."

"Boss, this whole process is calculated to make honest men act like felons. Sooner we all absorb that, the better."

Lanny simply saw more of what was going on than others did, more of the political tableau. They were all charged up about the beautiful Rembrandt detail; he had gone to the museum and seen the whole canvas. He was more aware, like a great basketball player who knows everything that's happening on the court.

The first time Casey took me turkey hunting, in Columbia County, we were sitting under the same tree. He saw three different birds coming through the woods, two hundred yards before I did. I was looking at the trees one at a time, and Casey somehow had his eyes wider open, took in the stereoscopic view. As I got more experience, I found I could do the same thing.

I came to realize over time that in a political campaign, the veteran infantryman's defensive squint counts for very little. Far more important to keep your eyes open wide on the horizon. Turkey hunting, like the theater, is good practice for politics.

The second week in July, Fay and St. Onge burst into my office at the New Courthouse, unable to contain themselves. "DA, you're gonna *love* this!" cackled Fay, throwing a tape on the table. I noted the official BPD markings, signaling this was from an undercover wiretap.

"What is it?" I asked.

"Seems Dellenbach's main guy, Colin Hanson, has quite an appetite for the young lads. Seems he even likes to be dominated, particularly when things don't go well. Seems the lads enjoy illicit substances. Seems Colin also talks much too much about his boss's Senate race, particularly when he has stumbled into the middle of an undercover narcotics investigation, as he has."

"Whew!" I exhaled. "I thought Washington, D.C.,

was the town where there are no secrets, not Boston. It took Boston to pry this out? Nice work. But, anyway, we can't use this stuff."

"Whaaat?"

"It's illegal, Jimmy," I said. "Black letter law. Criminal violation to use. In the ordinary course, this stuff would never see the light of day for another nine months. You know it, I know it. Plus, I don't like the karma. I'm not running against Colin Hanson. I've always thought he was pathetic, anyway. Who cares?"

"Terry, Dellenbach is one of the biggest gay-bashers in the United States Congress. This will kill him."

"No sale." I didn't look at Lanny.

As soon as Fay and St. Onge had left in disgust, Lanny turned to me calmly.

"Before you develop too much fellow feeling for your good pal Dellenbach, got some intelligence for you."

"What's that?"

"Press tells me, deep background, Dellenbach's goons are all over New York City, trying to dig up dirt on Rudy Solano's record in Brooklyn and Manhattan. Even trundled out an official U.S. Senate investigator—on his spare time, of course."

"That slippery bastard, you need two gloves and sand to hold him. Can we get the press to blow the whistle on him using, misusing, government resources?"

"Doubt it. Press would think it has the same stake as Dellenbach in seeing that whatever's there comes out. Press has high tolerance for sleazy investigative techniques by others."

"Lucky thing, too," I opined. Lanny laughed.

"May not be exactly where we want to hang the lantern anyway, Boss." Lanny paused. "I came in here on another question, a, uh, related but different question."

"What's that?"

"What are they, uh, what might they be likely to find? Possibly find. Hypothetically."

Spoken like a veteran practitioner of the criminal law, I thought.

"What do you mean? About what? You want to know what negative stuff they're likely to turn up on Rudy's record in New York?"

"That's correct."

"Nothing, that's what." Meaning, nothing I can tell you, anyway. What else could I say? This business really does make honest men act like felons.

"Okay, only checking. Always better to be prepared, just in case. I'll let them know."

Lanny was a pro. I went back to reading my stack of prosecution memos.

No good deed goes unpunished. The next week, Addie Stephens returned once again to the image of "the free-spending District Attorney, who makes $66,000 a year but lives in a million-dollar Back Bay town house and is always quick to spring for the check and hefty tips at the most posh establishments in town." Lanny and I didn't like the innuendo of that one, but we didn't think anyone really believed I was stealing their money and we liked the part about being a big tipper—which was true—so we let it ride. "Besides," said Lanny, "'I am not a crook' has been tried as a campaign theme, and it doesn't work." Opposite of our reaction to the integrity attack in the DA's race, but I was satisfied we were right both times. Matter of degree, common sense.

The next shot from the *Daily Mail*, however, caused me a rare loss of equanimity toward the press. Their resident right-wing columnist wrote a "news analysis" piece for page one, reporting that according to "sources who requested anonymity," there had been "rumors" in the New York Police Department that Detective Lieutenant Solano had taken money from narcotics defendants in the 1980s and had even been complicit in the unsolved death of a drug dealer. This columnist—or calumnist, as Emma called him—was well known to take dictation from Harold Dellenbach's press secretary, so none of us was surprised at the "request for anonymity."

Lanny was for going straight to the publisher or to this guy's boss, the editor of the editorial page. Jerry had a different take.

"Your problem isn't with the editorial page. When someone's writing as a columnist, you can't complain that they have an opinion. That's what the editorial page is for. Your problem is this guy's pretending to write a news story, and your decision maker there is either the managing editor or the city editor, I'll find out which."

Jerry did her homework, and she and I wound up having a little talk with the city editor, a longtime pal of the columnist. Actually, neither he nor I said anything.

"BULLSHIT, Greenie! You've got about sixty inches in two columns on page one, *yards* above the fold, and you say it's okay because you gave our point of view on the *jump* page? The jump page was in the furshlugginer *food* section, for Chrissake, nobody could've turned to it if they *wanted to* without knocking down three other people on the subway! And not that they would've felt they *needed to*, after that hatchet work on page *one!* Let me tell you, Green One, the fastest way to get to *be* a second-rank newspaper is to *act like* a second-rank newspaper!"

I was as glad to get out of the room as the city editor was. Jerry was pure plutonium, and I still wanted to have kids. "Later for you," she snarled over her shoulder as she stalked out.

That very day, Jerry leaked a major story, a luscious story about a corruption investigation, to the *New York Times*, on an exclusive basis. I asked her why not leak to the crosstown rival instead. "The *Daily Mail* never admits to itself it got beat by the *Gazette*, even when it does," Jerry explained. "The *Times* scoop will hurt Greenwood more. He'll have to explain it to the white wine and Brie crowd, which he hates to do." She paused, for breath only. "Right now, I wouldn't cross the street to piss on that guy if his coat was on fire."

I made a note not to get on Jerry's bad side.

Lanny and Jerry were sources of joy, throughout the summer and fall. They made me love the game. I was not surprised when, on October 9, we had closed to within eight points of our quarry in the *Daily Mail* tracking poll.

chapter nineteen

Mackerel by Moonlight

The rest of the month was extremely hot and heavy. The final televised debate was October 26, 1998, in a high school auditorium closer to Gardner, Mass., than we would have liked. That morning, the *Gazette* had us four points down, the *Daily Mail* had us three points up. Smart money consensus was it was going to be ours to lose.

Dellenbach's people evidently sensed this, because he came out of his crouch at the opening bell and swung wildly all night.

First he went after me on the Defense of Marriage Act, asking indignantly how I could refuse to support the cornerstone of Western and indeed human civilization. For an instant, I was tempted to argue the merits with him, but I remembered I wanted to win too much, so I got my game face back on. I explained this was merely a legal matter, of course I considered the union between man and woman sacrosanct. I was not in favor of gay marriage, I would not support it in Massachusetts, merely that the Full Faith and Credit Clause of the U.S. Constitution obliged us to observe the judicial acts of other states, same as a Reno, Nevada, divorce.

What I did not add is that coming from a known lecher whose campaign manager was one of the most accomplished pederasts in Washington, D.C., this was a breathtaking assault. In retrospect, I think they were hoping I would get into that, so that they could scream foul. Always change a losing game, as the sports coaches say.

I have to hand it to Dellenbach. With his seat on the line, and possibly the Republicans' majority in the U.S. Senate with it, he reached back down home country for the fastball, and he caught the plate a few times on me. I guess you don't get eighteen years in the Senate by accident.

He was all over me on the problems in the inner city, the crack babies, illegitimacy, and so on. It was all my fault. This got under my skin a little bit, and I made the mistake of coming back with some logical stuff: I could see his argument taking shape, it was a pyramid, the only problem was it was an inverted pyramid, and the point on which it rested was false, for the following reasons, et cetera.

Even as I was saying these words, I was thinking to myself, Rookie mistake. As long as you are talking about what he wants to talk about, no matter what you say, you are losing. Ever since Nixon and Agnew locked up the law and order issue in '68, Republicans everywhere have loved to talk about crime. Also, I could tell I was being too abstract.

Then Dellenbach went right at my record in office on corruption and white-collar crime cases. This was a type of maneuver that Lanny and I both admired. Making your own weakest point a strength: it's a variant of "hanging a lantern on your problem." With a million TV sets on, the second-to-second psychodynamics—the dial readings of two million viewers—are far more important than even the assessment of the media pundits. It wouldn't matter if Dan Watkins defended me in print the next day; what mattered is how did I *look*, right here, right now. This was the trench where the war would be fought and won or lost, and I did not like the way it was going.

Dellenbach rehearsed the by-now familiar criticism that the bank and money-laundering prosecutions had been superficial and wide of the mark. He implied that while we were fooling around with these little pieces of paper, *real* criminals were committing violent offenses and walking away. This was ridiculous and we both knew it, but for the casual viewer who hadn't followed the race, I wondered. . . .

Dellenbach plunged on, taking it up a notch and two. First he made a reference to the sour grapes criticism of my police corruption cases in New York. He had to know the press had already decided this was stale. I couldn't figure out whether he was trying to bring in the carpetbagger issue through the side door or whether he was just desperate to throw any mud he could. Then I remembered a lot of people were tuning in tonight for the first time.

It soon became evident this was all part of a plan

to stampede me. Dellenbach's language leapt to new heights, and as he reviewed my shortcomings in office, he worked himself up to his peroration: "Your record, sir, resembles a rotting mackerel by moonlight: it shines and it stinks."

I laughed out loud. As I well knew, these histrionics were not even original—the whole line was a John Randolph put-down of Livingston, two centuries ago. The pomposity, though, was vintage Dellenbach. I allowed myself a smug smile.

Unfortunately, while I was thinking these wise thoughts to myself, I wasn't saying anything out loud, and a two-million-viewer TV audience is an unfriendly backdrop for dead air. But at least I laughed, and Lanny and Jerry told me in the green room afterward that my "shoulder language" was good, that is, I was relaxed and enjoying myself. Probably thinking how smart I was to recognize the quote. Expensive self-indulgence.

Senator Dellenbach had saved a long-shot haymaker for last. They really must have thought they were going to lose by a mile.

He recounted the sad circumstances of Detective Lieutenant Rudy Solano's death, noted how much he hated even to bring it up—wink, wink!—then said, "And I have one final question for you, Mr. District Attorney, if you don't mind."

"Of course I don't mind," I replied amiably. "What is your question?"

"There was a published report in a prominent newspaper in this city that Officer Solano was suspected of corruption during the time he worked with you in New York City in the 1980s. You yourself argued at the coroner's inquest that his death might not have been suicide. Will you share with the audience the entire basis for your belief that your former colleague might not have taken his own life?"

I came completely unglued. "Senator," I blurted, "I hardly know where to start. You dishonor the memory of a brave police officer who is not here to defend himself. You have apparently sent your minions to review every facet of his distinguished thirty-year career in law enforcement"—I regretted this jab immediately, since I saw it would only prolong the discussion of an issue where I was on defense all the way—"and, of course, you found nothing. So now you desperately seek to muddy the circumstances of Lieutenant Solano's death, hoping to besmirch me in the process."

"My minions? My minions? It is you, sir, not I, who worked with this man, on whom the shadow of suspicion fell, and who has now died by his own hand, despite your suggestion to the contrary. It is you, sir, who owe it to this audience to explain all you know about the background of the deceased individual."

I knew damn well Dellenbach's researchers had come up empty because if he'd found anything, he would certainly have used it now. So I contented myself with defending Rudy's honor, and telling a couple of stories, fortunately true, about great cases he had developed as an investigator. But the whole unwieldy topic dominated the second half of the debate. I could see in Lanny's face afterward that he felt I had lost ground, despite the patent unfairness of Dellenbach's tactics. Since he had not really alleged anything, there was nothing for our rapid-response Truth Squad to operate on.

The papers the next morning were not as bad as I had feared, but I was still hot. I was off to see Brad Parmelee, the publisher of the *Daily Mail*, at 7:00 A.M., and I was carrying my long knife. He was already in his office. This was show time for everybody.

"Brother Parmelee, they are trying to *steal* this one—in broad daylight, with a pistol carved out of soap. This is a complete smear effort, and everybody in town knows it. Even worse, it was made possible by your own goddamn columnist writing a 'news' article with no sources other than Dellenbach himself, off the record. You can't let them do it. You cannot let them do it. You know Dellenbach, whatever his historical accomplishments, will be a whore for the Republicans whenever they need him. Without meaning to over-dramatize, the stakes are high here. I can't scream bloody murder during a televised debate, but some-body has to draw a line."

Parmelee listened intently, so much so that for once his hands didn't even flutter in mimicry around his butterfly bow tie. I felt I had made my point. In fact, I thought we were going to be all set.

I had felt I was all set before, though, only to have my world come apart.

chapter twenty

The Joy of the Hunt

It was smooth as silk of Rudy to tell me about the reopened murder investigation in front of the whole senior staff. I had to admire that. What better proof that this was business in the ordinary course, nothing to hide? I love a pro. I later drew on that move for inspiration, when I kept insisting Rudy could never have committed suicide. Misdirection is the greatest. Covers a multitude of sins. It was really too bad Rudy cracked.

Of course I knew exactly where Rudy was going to get the fresh air in his lungs that weekend in November. I had helped him field-dress his ten-pointer there two seasons earlier. His camp in Jaffrey was thirty miles almost dead north of Dana, Massachusetts, right on the same road. Route 202. I had the map in my mind.

I knew, too, that Rudy had never broken off contact with Olie Wing, even after the killings at the On Leong clubhouse in New York. Olie was simply too valuable a source of information. Once Rudy and Slifka let him go the first time, he would do anything for them. And with Slifka gone, Rudy had the asset all to himself.

I had always harbored suspicions about the "official" Hong Kong police report on Elijah Low's death: that the BMW had crashed on such a remote peninsula, fire had destroyed all evidence of the causes of death. I thought it might have had more to do with the greenness of certain currency than with the remoteness of the peninsula. Any doubt I had on this score was removed when the new regime in Hong Kong reopened the case: a .22-caliber entry wound is hard for a trained investigator to miss.

When Rudy as much as said to me in my office that he felt I had commissioned, or at the very least acquiesced in, the killing of Emma's husband, I knew I had to talk to him. After I saw him going to pieces before my eyes, shaking and sweating, I knew I had to help him think everything through, as he put it. Otherwise, there was no telling what he might say or do. He could do lasting harm to himself, he could do lasting harm to me. One thing I was sure of: cops don't like to go to jail. They'd sooner roll over on somebody. Just like my clients in the Metaxas case. Just like Joe Balls.

I was glad Rudy and I would have a coming to terms. I thought we could handle the whole thing in half an hour.

I knew the Blazer could get up to Jaffrey and back in well under four hours, and I was not worried about Emma waking up, after a full meal with red and white wine and two stingers.

The one scare was Parrish, pointing out in front of the media that I had fancy shoes on for the snowy woods on Saturday night. That's precisely why I wanted Gatto over to the town house so damn fast, so I could say I had no time to change. *Sure* I forgot those boots, Chester. Just what I wanted: arrive at the scene in a pair of boots that's *already* soaking wet. Those boots were locked up so tight and covered so deep with other stuff in my outdoor gear closet, they probably would've been dry by the time you found them anyway, you jerk.

I judged it to be in my best interest to push the second-hunter theory in public. A little fake handoff never hurts. Most people were sure it was suicide anyway. They think, Hey, .308 shot, .308 rifle, middle of the night—shot must've come from the rifle, right? People are not always all that attentive. Even medical examiners are not always that attentive, although with no slug retrieved and a point-blank wound, the ME didn't have much cause for curiosity. The coroner's jury finding of suicide merely confirmed what the world already knew.

Once I found Rudy's Tahoe, I knew which stands he'd be heading for. Rudy liked to sit on stands, whereas I like to prowl. But like me, he did favor getting out there early.

I wanted the advantage of surprise on my side. I wasn't clear what the endgame was going to be, but I wanted to make sure that whatever it was, I would be the one to choose it.

After I struck out on the first stand, I was pretty sure I could intercept Rudy before he set up in the second. And, sure enough, I made him out against the snow on the ground when he was maybe eighty yards from the stand, halfway up the hill. He was on snowshoes, moving slowly up a narrow defile between a thick patch of tag alders on the left and a stand of tall pines on the right. There was no moon. I cradled my .308 and moved fast up to his right, into the pines, then doubled back toward him. When I was about ten yards away, I called out his name. It was three or three-thirty and pitch black, the snow blotting out the stars and muffling sounds.

"Who's that?" he cried. I could see him tense, stumble a few steps away from me in his snowshoes, bend down, and try to peer above him into the blackness of the pines. Then he stumbled again.

"It's Terry, Terry Mullally," I said. "We need to talk. We need to talk everything through, to make sure no one gets hurt. I need to ask you a couple of questions."

"Oh, yeah? Whadda questions?" I saw Rudy lose his balance completely and crash into the alders. I realized he was drunk. It looked as though he was lying on his back, but I wasn't sure.

"Tell me more about Olie Wing. Tell me about Elijah Low."

"My guys found Olie inna whorehouse in Bangkok. Piece a cake. Old Olie got some of his money back! Outta my share, too. Shlifka's gone, and I din't bother you."

"Why are you so worried Olie will roll over on you?"

"Ah hah hah hah, thass *rich!* I can think of about two hunnert seventy thousand reasons, and ninety thousand of them you should unnerstan very well. I hear you did good with it in the market, too."

"Rudy, you know damn well that wasn't my idea. That was you and Paul all the way. You roped me in once, just one time, when I was in a bad way, but you made a goddamn career of it! You were behind all those cases, even Operation Submarine! You just used me."

"Mutual use, kid, purest and bes' form of politics. But, sure, of course I unnerstan, you're not very pregnant. Maybe take you ten months to have a kid, 'stead of nine."

"Goddamn it, thanks to you we had no case on Olie. He would've walked anyway. You and Slifka screwed up the search."

"Sure, that's what you said, to make yourself feel better, after we split up the dough. We had him dead to rights, two police eyewitnesses. If you hadn't been the duty attorney that night, Olie'd still be in MCC–New York."

"But it was a good law enforcement move. We were developing him to use in other cases, *remember?*"

"Yeah, like you getting him to take out your girlfriend's homeboy!"

"That's not true, don't say that!"

"Why? You afraid I'm wearing a wire? Hanhh, hah, hah."

"It never happened! It didn't happen!" I shouted. I had to shout. The wind was picking up.

"So that's your story and you're sticking with it,

huh, Terry? 'It never happened.' I guess the apple don't fall far from the tree."

"What the hell do you mean by that?"

"I mean like father, like son, kid. Your old man played it both ways for years. And let me tell you something else, you're not going to leave me hanging out to dry on this one, not on this one, not by a long shot."

He had staggered to his feet, leaning on a small alder, and now dropped to his knees. I saw him release the safety and point the Savage almost directly at me. Complete chance. I was sure he couldn't see me at all in among the pines.

"You forgot where you came from, Terry," he said hoarsely.

"That's *enough!*" I shouted.

The darkness and silence were split by a scream as the round from Rudy's .308 blew past me, a couple of feet to my right. Warning shot, or drunk shot? I moved quickly forward to get behind a big pine.

Through a crook of the tree, I could see Rudy's bulk against the snow of the hill; he couldn't hide his frame behind those two-inch saplings. He was down in a crouch, not twenty feet from me. I couldn't see his gun, which meant it was probably still pointed in my direction. I kept squinting hard at Rudy's outline. The snow was getting in my eyes, but I kept motionless.

My mind was elsewhere. People, leaves, distance, light, depth, time . . . I thought of my eight-year-old father running along the lane behind his house in Dana, standing on tiptoe to pick apples, having his father hold him up, laughing. . . . I thought of my father, holding me up on the windowsill, putting both arms around me. I thought of holding Emma, in her baggy blue sweater, at the Quabbin, gliding over Dana. I realized Rudy was going to take all that away from me—either right here with his rifle, or later, more slowly, in court.

From behind the pine, I shouted, "You're a dead man when Olie rolls over on you, Rudy. Cops like you don't do well in the joint."

Rudy screamed, "No!"

He stood up suddenly. I momentarily lost him in the snow. I heard his snowshoe break through a crust of snow. Once. Then again, closer. I stepped to the side so I would have a clear swing if I needed it. I thought I heard a crunch just yards away.

I never heard the second shot.

Rudy's outline spun around, then sank and slumped onto his gun. I waited a full minute, but there was no further movement.

"See you in church," I said finally. And I did. Many people said my oration at the memorial service for Rudy was the best speech I gave in calendar 1998. And 1998 was a good year.

With the exuberant blessing of the Church and the laity of Boston, Emma and I got married at St. Margaret's in December, just before moving to Washington.

Washington, the town with no secrets.

The End